"Look at me, Noelle," Colby said quietly. Slowly she lifted her head until she was staring into his eyes. And in the shimmering reflection of the skyline lights she could see a fire flickering amid the green depths. The sight started a burning deep within her body. "What is it?" she whispered.

"When you signed that contract, you became my client. But the minute I met you, you became much more." He lowered his head, bringing his mouth tantalizingly close to hers, and when he spoke his voice was rough. "It took about two blinks of those brown eyes for me to begin to crave you in the worst possible way."

His breath fanned over her lips, heating her inside and out. Without thinking, she went up on her toes and lightly touched her mouth to his.

He could barely call it a kiss, but it sent a bolt of electricity through him. Then she did it again, and he forgot everything but the taste of her lips as he pulled her into his arms.

She was consumed with a hot hunger that burned reason right out of her. He tasted like desire. He tasted like need. And all she knew was that she wanted more. . . .

WHAT ARE *LOVESWEPT* ROMANCES?

They are stories of true romance and touching emotion. We believe those two very important ingredients are constants in our highly sensual and very believable stories in the *LOVESWEPT* line. Our goal is to give you, the reader, stories of consistently high quality that may sometimes make you laugh, sometimes make you cry, but are always fresh and creative and contain many delightful surprises within their pages.

Most romance fans read an enormous number of books. Those they truly love, they keep. Others may be traded with friends and soon forgotten. We hope that each *LOVESWEPT* romance will be a treasure—a "keeper." We will always try to publish

LOVE STORIES YOU'LL NEVER FORGET
BY AUTHORS YOU'LL ALWAYS REMEMBER

The Editors

Loveswept

Fayrene Preston
Caprice

BANTAM BOOKS

NEW YORK · TORONTO · LONDON · SYDNEY · AUCKLAND

CAPRICE

A Bantam Book / Special Edition—Not for Sale

PUBLISHING HISTORY
Bantam edition published March 1993
Bantam reissue / September 1994

If you would be interested in receiving protective vinyl covers for your
Loveswept books, please write to this address for information:

Loveswept
Bantam Books
P.O. Box 985
Hicksville, NY 11802

ISBN 0-553-19939-0

Published simultaneously in the United States and Canada

PRINTED IN THE UNITED STATES OF AMERICA

OPM   0 9 8 7 6 5 4 3

Many thanks to Charles Horie for his help regarding police procedure.

One

Noelle Durrell

The name in script above the door of her exclusive North Dallas boutique always made Noelle smile. Still. Even after five years.

But this morning as she crossed the parking lot to the sidewalk in front of her shop, Noelle wasn't smiling. A mannequin in her big display window had fallen over. Dressed in a sequined chiffon dress with a low neck and back, the mannequin was leaning drunkenly against a second mannequin that displayed a sexy red number. A third mannequin was sprawled on the floor.

"Looks like someone threw a party and didn't invite me," Noelle muttered, baffled, as she slipped her key into the lock and went in. There had to be a perfectly good explanation, though at the moment she couldn't imagine what it might be.

She started through the boutique, but almost at once came to an abrupt stop. Something was wrong. Very wrong. Garments were strewn on the floor, cottons on top of sequins, rayons on top of chiffons. It was as if someone had been hurrying by and knocked them from the racks. And the usually perfectly arranged jewelry in the glass display cases was in a jumble. Stone necklaces were tangled, and earrings rested on their sides or facedown.

"Oh hell," she murmured, "I've been robbed."

She should leave, she thought, her mind racing. Hadn't she heard or read that if a place had been robbed, you should get out fast and go elsewhere to call 911 in case the burglar was still on the premises? So, all right, she should leave. Except—

Dammit, this was her shop. She had worked hard to build this business. Financing it with money inherited from her grandmother, she had used her love of fashion, business acumen, and instinctive good taste to build a loyal clientele. And she wasn't going to be run out of it by some punk looking for drug money. In fact, she thought, reaching with both hands for a good-size, satisfyingly heavy ornamental vase, she hoped she ran into the worm.

Psyched for a round or two with the thugs who had done this to her beautiful shop, she was disappointed to reach her office without encountering anyone. She punched out 911 and gave the operator the pertinent information. Then, after a moment's thought, she dialed the number for the Brennan Security Agency.

Officer David Hogan watched Noelle pace in front of him. Being happily married for nearly ten years hadn't diminished his ability to appreciate a good-looking woman, and Noelle Durrell was extraordinarily lovely with her big dark eyes and cloud of sable-brown hair. She was wearing a knockout of a suit, too. Deep pink, with a tight, short skirt, it would look great on his wife. Of course, after three kids his wife didn't quite have Miss Durrell's figure, but then he supposed it didn't matter. He probably wouldn't be able to afford the suit anyway.

"I left here around six-thirty yesterday evening," she said, at last answering his question, "and I didn't return until nine-thirty this morning." She stopped and shot him a piercing look. "Shouldn't you be dusting for fingerprints or something?"

"No, ma'am. Someone from the Physical Evidence Department will do that. They may be able to get prints off the jewelry cases or the back door."

Noelle rolled her eyes. "It'll be just my luck that whoever did this watches television and knew to wear gloves. Watch television long enough and you can learn anything. I suppose I'll have to keep the store closed until they're through dusting?"

"I'm afraid so."

"Damn."

She touched the quartz necklace at her throat, and he noted the slight tremor in her hand. Being upset was normal, he thought, but she was also angry. In his experience a little anger was a healthy sign. It was the people who withdrew and got too quiet who worried him.

"Who else had access to your store, Miss Durrell?

"No one."

"What about a cleaning crew? Or repairmen?"

"I'm always here when repairs are done, and the cleaning service isn't scheduled for three days. Someone from the security agency lets them in and then locks up after they're gone."

"And you're sure no one else has access? Employees, for instance?"

"I have two part-time employees, Grace and Joy Williams—they're sisters—but I've never given them a key. There's never been any need. I'm always the first to arrive and the last to leave."

"Have you had a chance to determine what's missing?"

She shook her head. "I don't think any clothes have been taken, but I can't be sure until I do a more thorough check. They did clean out my cash box in the back and got a *whole* twenty-five dollars for their considerable trouble."

"Do you usually keep more cash than that on hand?"

"Not really. There's no need to. And if they, whoever the hell they are, had given the matter any thought, they would have realized it. My kind of business deals mostly in checks and credit cards." She couldn't keep the irritation from her voice. This break-in seemed so senseless. She couldn't understand it, and because she didn't, it made her want to scream. Granted, it didn't look as if she had lost anything of great value, and with an hour's work and a new lock on the back door no one would be able to tell the shop had been broken into. But she had very proprietary feelings about her boutique, and whoever had broken in had scraped a nerve.

Finishing a notation in his notebook, Officer Hogan nodded. "Anything else?"

She glanced toward the jewelry cases. "I don't carry real jewelry, just extremely good costume jewelry. I do carry some gold, and it looks as if they might have taken several pairs of the gold earrings, but that's it. What in the world do you think they had in mind?"

"Maybe they thought you carried the real stuff."

"Then their IQ must register in the low double digits. I sell clothing, not jewelry." She gave an exclamation of annoyance. "Dammit, why *my* shop? I pay a fortune for security. Someone must have really been asleep at the switch."

"I can personally guarantee you that no one was asleep at the switch," a deep voice behind her said.

She whirled to see a tall man with thick, wheat-colored hair and the coolest, darkest green eyes she had ever seen. She was stunned. It flashed through her mind that he would be a good thief, because she hadn't even heard the door open. And in his white open-necked shirt, pressed jeans, light-colored sports jacket, and black lizardskin boots, this man looked like someone who wouldn't hesitate to take what he wanted whether it belonged to him or not. Something cold, then warm, shimmied up her spine.

"I'm also in a position to know that you don't pay a fortune. In fact, what you pay is very reasonable." He held out his hand. "I'm Colby Brennan, owner of Brennan Security."

She automatically extended her hand toward him, but when she felt his hand close strongly around hers, she jerked away. Suddenly she had someone on whom she could focus her anger. "You show up *now*, at ten in the morning? Where were you last night when my shop was being burglarized?"

"I can understand why you're upset. I'm not thrilled myself."

"Who cares? The fact is, I pay you for security services, and you didn't do your job." She could have been throwing shadows at him for all the reaction her anger caused.

"As I said," he murmured, "I can understand why you're upset." He turned to the policeman. "Hi. Colby Brennan. Have you figured out when this happened?"

"Sometime between six-thirty last night and nine-thirty this morning is the best we can do."

Colby shook his head. "Somehow they bypassed our security system. The alarm didn't trigger."

"*Then*," Noelle said through clenched teeth, "I would say that what I pay you isn't reasonable at all—not if some kid can waltz in and out of here undetected and do this to my shop."

Colby shifted his gaze back to her, and though his demeanor remained calm, Noelle saw something in his eyes she had missed before, a hard, dangerous light that caused her a moment's unease.

"If it was a kid," he said softly, "then he was an extremely smart kid."

In her peripheral vision she saw Officer Hogan nodding in agreement. She forgot the unease as her anger surged back, stronger than ever. "A smart kid wouldn't have broken into a boutique expecting to find money."

He looked at her thoughtfully. "Then it seems we have a mystery on our hands. Do you like mysteries, Miss Durrell?"

"Only in books, Mr. Brennan."

Officer Hogan cleared his throat. "I believe I have all the information I need for now, Miss Durrell."

Noelle blinked, then focused on the officer, surprised that she had momentarily forgotten he was still there.

"An investigator will be assigned to your case and will be in touch, probably tomorrow. It would help if you could have a complete list of what was taken by then. Someone from Physical Evidence should be here within the next few hours. Try not to touch anything until then."

"Thank you, Officer Hogan," Noelle said, fighting for composure. "Tell me, how long does it usually take for cases like this one to be solved?"

He threw a quick glance at Colby Brennan. "It varies, depending on if there are any witnesses or if we are able to collect any tangible evidence, such as fingerprints."

"I see. Well, thank you."

Officer Hogan nodded and turned to go, but at the door he stopped and looked back. "By the way, Miss Durrell, does your store by any chance have a layaway plan?"

"Not really, but occasionally I'll make a special arrangement with one of my customers—why do you ask?"

"I was just thinking that my wife would look nice in a suit like the one you have on."

Noelle's heart softened, and she smiled. "Come in anytime. I'm sure we'll be able to work something out." The smile was still on her face when she looked back at Colby Brennan.

"Very nice," he murmured, taking in the alluring

warmth in her eyes and the sweetness in the curve of her lips. "Smiling becomes you."

The smile faded. She didn't know whether it was because of the burglary or because of him, but suddenly she realized that she felt decidedly undone and unprepared, as if she'd forgotten to put on her lipstick or as if her slip was showing. She touched one of the quartz stones of the necklace she wore, betraying her nerves. "What was that look you and Officer Hogan exchanged? What is it you both know that Officer Hogan didn't want to tell me?"

His green eyes glittered approvingly. "You're very sharp, Miss Durrell."

"And *you're* very condescending."

"I apologize. I didn't mean to be."

For some reason his obviously genuine sincerity irritated her further. She tried to shrug it away. "Well? What do you both know? I asked *you* the question because I wasn't sure Officer Hogan would tell me."

"And you think I will?"

"I do employ you."

A very neat put-down, he reflected. And he supposed he needed it, a reality check to remind him that she was a client. But remembering wasn't easy. Even though he'd known her only minutes, he was finding it a struggle to keep a professional objectivity about her. Emotion lit her brown eyes with gold streaks, and high color tinged her delicate features.

"I'm very aware that you employ me, but do you have to keep calling me Mr. Brennan? I'd like to call you Noelle. It might make this situation a little easier."

Easier for whom? she wanted to ask. He said her name in a voice that sounded like rough velvet and made her pulses react crazily. She could no longer chalk up her reaction to the burglary alone, and she really hated that she couldn't. "Please, just answer my question."

"Sure. Here it is. Unless an eyewitness or some pretty substantial evidence is found, this case probably won't get solved by the police. The Physical Evidence Department will come out here this afternoon and try to find prints or something the person or persons might have left behind, but chances are pretty good they won't find anything. The investigator will come out tomorrow and ask you the same questions Officer Hogan asked. He'll also try to find the time to nose around the shopping center to see if anyone might have seen something, but chances are equally good no one did. And then he will write *Suspend case pending further information* at the bottom of your file, and go on to the next case. Their caseload is simply too high to spend much time on cases that are dead ends."

"And this burglary is a dead end?"

"No one can say that for certain yet."

Much as she hated to admit it, his account of what would happen made sense. But that was the only thing currently making sense to her. "Mr. Brennan—"

"Please, call me Colby."

She didn't want to call him anything. Instinct told her it would be risky to get too familiar with him. He was standing between her and the front of the shop so that his broad shoulders partially blocked from her view the light coming through the windows. Shadows delineated his face, but she had no trouble seeing the hard lines of his features and the sensual fullness of his lips. His gaze was both penetrating and compelling, and in the exclusively feminine surroundings, his bold masculinity was magnified tenfold. She took a deep, steadying breath and clasped her hands together. "Look, there's no need for you to stay any longer."

Acid churned in his gut at her dismissal. She was all business, a mirror image of his normal behavior. But she was also magnetically beautiful, with lips that seemed incredibly sweet and brown velvet eyes that made him wonder how soft they would look after a night of lovemaking. Everything in him wanted to say to hell with professionalism. It was a dementia he couldn't explain. "I think there's every need for me to stay."

"Not really. Nothing much was taken, and no one was hurt. Just forget it. And, listen, I'm sorry if I've been rude."

Now she was apologizing to him. He liked her better when her eyes flashed fiery anger. Much better. The fire hinted that passions lay simmering beneath the businesslike veneer she presented. How *deep* was the question that interested him.

His silence pounded against her ears. His dark green gaze burned her skin. Her nerves began to fray. "I haven't had a very good day so far," she said in an attempt to explain her rudeness, "and it doesn't seem to be getting any better."

"I know you haven't." She had beautiful skin, white with a delicate pink undertone. He wanted to touch her, brush his fingers along her cheek, a gesture to reassure her everything would be all right. But she wouldn't welcome his touch, and he wasn't sure he could keep it reassuring. "And you blame me for everything."

In spite of her best intentions her anger resurfaced. And the thing was, she *hated* being angry. "Not quite everything. Not for toxic waste or world hunger. But for what happened here, yes, I do. Two months ago I, along with every other business person in this shopping center, had a meeting concerning the rash of burglaries that have been occurring in the area. We elected three representatives to do research on security firms. I was out of town on a buying trip when you made your presentation—"

"I knew I hadn't seen you before. I wouldn't have forgotten you."

Ignore it, she told herself. Just ignore it. She fixed him with a stern gaze. "But our representatives recommended you, and on the basis of that recommendation I signed a contract and sent you a check. By taking those actions, I *thought* I was protecting my shop. You were supposed to keep anyone from breaking in."

He had the urge to laugh, but only at himself. She was attacking both him and what he did, and his instinct was to be defensive. Yet his body had another agenda entirely—he was beginning to crave her. "Security systems are designed and run by people, Noelle, and people aren't perfect. The best security system in the world can be circumvented if someone is smart enough and determined enough. My system is damned good. Whoever broke in here was both smart *and* determined."

Which brought them back to square one, she thought ruefully. It didn't make sense.

"Stop worrying," he said softly.

She looked at him in surprise. "What makes you think I'm worrying?"

"You're not smiling."

He threatened her in a very basic way. Somewhere deep inside her she had a feeling she knew why, but she shied away from exploring that reason. She shook her head, feeling helpless and frustrated.

"Believe it or not, I'm as upset about this as you are. You've ruined my perfect record."

Right, she thought. She was probably the first woman not to fall at his feet.

"I've been in the security business nine years. The system I installed in your place and others in the shopping center is relatively new. It took a lot of trial and error to perfect, and you're the first one of my clients using the new system who's been burglarized."

She blinked. *Burglarized.* She couldn't believe it, but she had momentarily forgotten what had happened to her boutique. She'd been thinking of *him.* "Lucky me."

"Actually you are, because I promise you, if there is any way to find out who did this, I will."

She looked at him blankly. "You?"

"Me. I have two things the police don't have—time and available manpower."

"No," she said firmly. "I told you to forget it."

His gaze dropped to the quartz necklace that clung to the base of her neck. Each large nugget was encased in a delicate cage of gold. The milky hue of the nuggets picked up the pink color of her suit and the blush undertone beneath her flawless skin. "I'm sorry," he said huskily, "but I can't forget."

His husky tone skimmed along her nerves, at once grating and soothing. It was with gratitude that she heard the front door open and turned to see Joy Williams saunter in, her waist length white-blond hair swinging, her spectacular slim young body showing off a Liz Claiborne slacks outfit to perfection.

"Hi," said Joy, quickly scanning the shop. Her gaze zeroed in on Colby. "What's going on?"

Noelle pushed tensed fingers through her hair. "The shop was burglarized during the night."

Joy's eyes widened. "Are you all right?"

Noelle smiled at her. "I'm fine, honey, and this is Colby Brennan, head of Brennan Security. Mr. Brennan, this is Joy, one of my employees."

Colby absorbed Noelle's tender smile at the girl with interest and an accelerated heartbeat. He had to force himself to turn away from her and greet the newcomer. "Hi, Joy. Nice to meet you."

"Nice to meet you too." She grinned, eyeing him in the frank, open way of the innocent and young. "So *you're* Colby Brennan. Well, I can certainly see why Maureen Jacobson was having such a fit over you. Her mother owns a shop in this shopping center, and Maureen went with her to hear your presentation. Ever since, she's been telling me what a hunk you are."

Noelle regarded Colby's amused expression with irritation. It couldn't be more obvious that he was used to women talking about him, calling him a hunk, and in the bargain probably drooling all over him. "*Joy*." As an attempt to get Joy to remember her manners, it failed.

Joy spared her a glance before she looked back at Colby. "It's true. Maureen said she was working in her mother's shop the other day when you came in with a very pretty lady."

Colby's brows drew together as he tried to remember. "What's the name of the shop?"

"The Brass and Candle Shop," Joy said. "It's on the south side of the shopping center. Maureen said the lady bought you three boxes of candles, and then you bought the candle holders."

His face cleared. "Now I remember. Kristie decided my place needed candles and insisted on buying me some, then I had to buy the candle holders to have something to put them in."

Lord but the man was annoying, Noelle thought. To her further irritation her stomach knotted at the idea of him with "a very pretty lady." But since Joy had introduced the subject, she didn't see any harm in following it up. "She sounds nice," she said in a half-questioning way that invited more comment.

His eyes cut to her. "She is. Very. Kristie's my sister."

"Oh."

Joy happily clapped her hands together. "I can't wait to tell Maureen. She saw the wedding band on her finger and decided that you were having an affair with a married woman."

Sister. Unaccountably Noelle's tension eased.

"Try to restrain your glee over getting one up on Maureen."

Joy giggled. "Sorry, but she's such a gossip. It will do her good to be told for once that she's wrong."

"Would you mind answering a few questions later on?" Colby asked Joy.

"No—"

A scratching sound on the glass of the front door interrupted them. Joy went to open the door, and a white toy poodle pranced in, his tail wagging, his eyes alight with interest. Two red plaid bows perched atop his ears, a slim red leather collar circled his neck, and at the first sight of Colby the dog raced to him.

"What is it?" Colby asked dubiously, his head bent as he watched the fluffy little fur ball sniff his boots.

"*Not* it, *he*. His name is Sottise." Noelle scooped him up in her arms. Then, because it was automatic to explain to new customers, she added, "His name is a French word that means something silly and frivolous."

"I believe it."

"Be careful, or you'll hurt his feelings." Joy reached out to give the dog an approving scratch on his neck and coo to him. "You look so cute with your little red plaid bows, sweetie pie." Sottise licked her hand.

"Why did he show up at the door? I mean, where did he come from?"

Noelle had to grin. The ultramasculine Colby Brennan was bewildered by a dog. So far the sight was the highlight of her day. "The groomers. They're at the end of the walkway. Sottise has an account there. Once a week I drop him off before I open the shop, and when he's through they let him out, and he runs down here."

"Funny," he said. "I would have figured you for a Doberman."

She arched a brow, a challenging gesture. "You don't like my dog?"

He smiled. "That's *not* a dog. It's a cotton ball with eyes and a tongue."

His smile was blatantly charming. She regarded it with distrust. "If I'd known your security system was so bad, I would have gotten a Doberman."

"Be careful, Noelle. A few more stab wounds and I'll be bleeding all over your carpet."

"I'll send you the cleaning bill."

Joy looked from one to the other with interest. "So do you want me to start picking up things or what?"

Noelle shook her head, not in answer, but because she was puzzled by her own behavior. The man could make her forget both subjects and people. "No. We have to leave everything just as it is, but you can help me figure out what jewelry was taken. We also need to check the clothes."

"That's going to take a while. I'll print out our inventory list and start to work. Oh, and Colby, you can question me any time you like. You can even frisk me."

His smile broadened. "It would be my pleasure, I'm sure."

Joy's blue eyes sparkled with good humor as she disappeared into a back room.

Even though she was only ten years older than Joy's nineteen years, Noelle suddenly felt as if several generations separated them. Never in a million years would she be able to duplicate Joy's spontaneity and ease with Colby. And, she reflected with disgust, she might as well admit what her problem with him was. Deep down she knew he was a man she could be attracted to if she only let herself, and as such, he represented everything she had gone out of her way to avoid these last few years. Just looking at him took an energy that drained the strength from her bones.

Never again, she thought. Never again.

"Joy's incorrigible," she murmured.

"She's delightful, and I *will* want to ask her a few questions later, but right now I have one for you."

Noelle was lost in thought. Maybe it was unfair, but she assumed that the burglar was a man. Officer Hogan certainly was a man. And Colby Brennan was most *definitely* male, intensely and powerfully. She felt an urgent need to reclaim her shop and her senses from all things male—and most particularly from Colby Brennan. He filled her store to the four corners with the sensuality of his presence until all she could think, see, or hear was him. She wanted him gone.

"I know what you said about the police department's handling of this case," she said finally, "but I'm willing to let them see what they can do."

"So am I, but in the meantime I'll be on the job."

"No—"

"*Noelle.*" He wanted her complete attention, and his stern tone got it. She looked up at him, startled. "Whoever came into this store got through *my* system, not the police department's. *My* system. Do you understand? That makes this break-in very personal to me."

She shut her eyes and drew a deep breath, then another. Then she opened her eyes. Dammit, as much as she'd like to, she couldn't fault him for his attitude. She sighed, deciding the sooner she answered his questions, the sooner he'd leave. "Okay, what do you want to know?"

"Has anyone odd or out of the ordinary come into the shop in the last week or two?"

While she considered his question, she put Sottise down and watched him run to investigate the clothes on the floor. "No, Sottise," she said quietly. Obediently he trotted over to a large blue satin pillow with a matching soft blue blanket and settled on top of it. "It depends on what you mean by *odd*. Quite a few of my customers could be called eccentric."

"I'm talking about anyone who wouldn't fit in with your normal clientele, someone you might have been surprised to see here."

"No. It's just been the usual crowd."

"Have you had any repair work done?"

"At my home, but not here."

"What did you have done at your home?"

"The exterior painted. The painters started this morning, and they'll be working on it for the next couple of days."

"Did you check their references before you hired them?"

"Of course I did, and they're the best."

"I'm not questioning your judgment, Noelle, simply looking for something that might give me a clue about who did this." His tone was gently chiding.

"Right. Sorry." It was a strange day, she reflected. She wished it were over, and it was only beginning.

"Does anyone have access to this store after hours beside yourself?"

"No one except the cleaning service, which one of your men lets in once a week."

He exhaled a long breath. She hadn't given him a thing he could work with. "Okay, I guess we'll have to wait and see if the police can come up with anything this afternoon. But like I said, don't worry I'm going to be checking around the shopping center to see if I can find someone who might know something."

"You're leaving?" Minutes before, she had wanted him gone, but now that he was about to leave, she felt a strange wrench.

His eyes glittered darkly. "Would you like me to stay?"

"No," she said quickly, *too* quickly. "There's no need," she added more slowly, infusing calm into her tone. "In fact, you know what? This has obviously been a mistake on someone's part. Who knows? Maybe they got the wrong address."

"Maybe, but I still can't let myself off the hook. You had every right to be angry with me. You paid me to protect your store, and I let you down. I owe it to you to see if I can find out who did it—plus, I need to figure out where my system failed. I'll be back when the Physical Evidence people show up."

He reached for her hand, taking it in his, knowing the proper thing to do would be to shake it, but instead simply holding it. Her hand was small and delicate, as she was, but he also felt a strength and competence in her fingers. She wore a slim watch and three dainty gold bracelets on her slender wrist. But there were no rings on her fingers. He had called her *Miss* Durrell, he realized. He had never met her before, but he had jumped to the conclusion that she was single, almost as if it was beyond him even to contemplate the possibility of her being married.

"Take care," he said softly.

And then he was gone, striding past the yellow daffodils growing in the planter by the door, out into the sunlight, across the parking lot.

Involuntarily she took several steps to her left so that she could keep him in her line of vision for a few seconds more. He was heading toward a sleek Jaguar, the same dark green color as his eyes. He moved with an ease and strength that spoke of athleticism, but there was something else . . . an almost imperceptible unevenness to his gait. Maybe he had twisted an ankle recently, she thought, then wondered why she was so interested. She wouldn't have noticed his uneven gait if she hadn't been studying him so closely. With a frown she went to find Joy.

Two

Colby strode into the command center of his company, his expression dark. Two of his men sat before a control panel and phone system that kept them apprised of problems with any of their various accounts. At least that was the way it was *supposed* to work.

"Hey, Colby." The greeting came from Ted Monroe, an older man with a hefty build who was a retired police officer. "How did it go at Noelle Durrell's? Did she fire us?"

Ted's question was asked facetiously, but Colby saw no humor in it. Since he knew Ted meant no harm, he kept his reply even. "Not yet, but if she had, I wouldn't blame her. Did you get hold of Kenny?"

"Sure did. He should be in any time now."

Kenny Jamison had been the security guard assigned to the shopping center the night before. He walked the area in a pattern that would have had him passing Noelle Durrell's shop every hour, and Colby was eager to talk to him.

"What about Rob?" Besides himself, Rob was his best electronics expert, and as soon as the call had come in about the break-in, he had set Rob on the problem of how their system could have been bypassed so neatly.

"Rob's on the job, but he hasn't found anything yet."

Just then Kenny walked in, his expression concerned. "Got your report with you?" Colby asked.

"Yes, sir, but I'm not sure what help either it or I can be. I didn't see a thing out of place last night. I didn't even notice anything wrong with that back door lock."

Colby grimaced. "It was a clever job all right, too clever to suit me." He had made it a point to check out the back lock before entering the store; to the naked eye, nothing looked wrong.

"Did Miss Durrell have any ideas?"

"She wants to think it was a mistake, that whoever did it really meant to hit some other place. *I'd* like to think that too."

"But you don't?"

"A couple of things bother me." He'd been referring to the break-in, but suddenly he was remembering Noelle's lovely dark eyes, how one minute they had blazed with anger, and the next minute they had lit with warmth. And he remembered how her lips had curved, sweet and tempting. One look at her, and he had wanted to take her to bed. Sweet hell, if only he'd met her under other circumstances.

"Okay, Kenny, let's step into my office. We're going to go over your report a minute at a time. Maybe it will jar your memory on something. And in the meantime, Ted, pull up the info on all our accounts. We may have a serious problem."

• • •

Noelle spent the morning checking her inventory and explaining to customers who showed up that she would be closed until late in the afternoon. She allowed a couple of her regulars in for coffee and speculation on what had happened. As usual Sottise went from one lady to another, enjoying the petting and attention he was paid. And when he got tired, he curled up in a chair beside one of them and went to sleep. There was certainly something to be said for a dog's life, Noelle thought wryly.

Around one o'clock two men from Physical Evidence showed up. Ten minutes later Colby walked in, and her defense system automatically kicked back into play.

To Noelle's surprise he greeted the two policemen warmly. "Hi, guys, how's it going?"

The tall man who had introduced himself to her as Officer Klein smiled broadly at Colby. "Not too bad. What about you? What's it like to live such a cushy life?"

"It's great, but the best part of it is, I don't have to look at your ugly mugs every day."

The other officer spoke up. "Oh, come on, Colby. You know you miss us. I'm surprised you've lasted this long without us."

"It's been a piece of cake. Besides, all of you seem to be doing just fine. I heard about the great work the unit did on that Hasseldorf case. Way to go."

"Sometimes the good guys do win," the second officer said. "Pretty friggin' amazing, huh?"

Colby nodded understandingly, then gestured around. "Anything show up yet?"

"We haven't been here that long, but so far nothing."

He nodded again. "Let me know, will you?"

"Sure thing."

Noelle had been watching him with the policemen, so she witnessed his easy, congenial manner vanish when he turned and crossed to her. There was a new tension in his body that hadn't been there moments before, an intensity in his gaze. She and he were like two pieces of flint, she concluded. Strike them together, and they would generate heated emotion. She didn't want any part of it.

"How are you?"

"Fine."

He searched her face and saw composure with a large portion of wariness. He wished for the anger back. From her, he'd rather have unguarded emotion. "Have you finished with the list of things that were stolen?"

She shrugged. "Twenty-five dollars, three pairs of gold earrings, and two pieces of costume jewelry."

"That's it?"

"That's it." She wrapped her arms around her waist, feeling the need to protect herself. "The costume jewelry is by Kenneth Kaye, and it's great stuff, but it's relatively inexpensive. I don't know—maybe they'll be able to sell the earrings for the gold."

Because he would have felt better if the burglars had behaved predictably and cleaned out the place, he kept his response light. "Either that or they have girlfriends they're trying to impress."

"If that was what they were after, they could have done a lot better. I carry clothes worth far more than those earrings." Despite herself, her guard slipped a fraction, and her lips quirked. "Maybe they didn't know what size their girlfriends wore and decided to go the safe route. Jewelry makes a nice gift, no matter what the occasion." She noticed Sottise edging closer to the two police officers. "Sottise, get back over here." He turned his head and looked at her as if to say, *Who, me?* "Now, Sottise." He trotted obediently to her side and looked up at her expectantly. "I told you to leave them alone." She pointed toward his bed. "Go lie down." With a barely audible sniff he did her bidding.

Her voice was soft and gentle when she spoke to the little dog, Colby reflected. He had also heard anger and wariness in her voice. But he couldn't help wondering what her voice would sound like urgent and ragged with need. Desire coiled low in his body, nearly driving him to his knees. Frustrated and trying his damnedest to get his mind off the effect she was having on him, he practically shouted at her. "Does he come to work with you every day?"

Unsure of this new mood of his, she regarded him more cautiously than ever. "He'd be heartbroken if I left him behind. Coming here is one of his greatest joys. My regular customers take on over him, and Grace and Joy spoil him rotten."

He stared into her deep brown eyes and nearly lost his train of thought. "I suppose he could grow on a person."

Curiosity got the better of her. "Don't you have a dog or a cat?"

"No. I'm allergic to them."

It struck her funny that such an obviously virile and strong man would have something as common and aggravating as an allergy, but she kept her humor to herself. "It's their hair. You should try a poodle. They have fur instead of hair and don't shed. Most people who can't tolerate being around a dog or a cat aren't bothered by poodles."

Tearing his gaze away from her, he glanced at the dog and saw that he was curled into a tight little ball, apparently already asleep. He looked like a powder puff topped by two red bows. "*Maybe* he could grow on a person, but as *what* I don't know. As I said, he's not a dog."

"Sottise would agree completely with you."

He looked back at her and saw that her lips were slightly curved. "Dammit but I like it when you smile."

Something sweet and hot melted through her, taking her completely off guard. She looked around for a distraction. Or a weapon with which to protect herself.

To hell with professionalism, Colby thought. Before this was all over, he would know if her lips were as sweet as they looked. Just then Joy walked by, her long white-blond hair swinging.

Joy was only a kid, and normally he wouldn't have given her a second's worth of attention, but circumstances made this situation different. First of all, she was associated with a woman who seemed to be becoming more important to him by the minute. Plus, at some point he was going to have to talk to her. But right now he simply needed to ease some of the tension between him and Noelle.

"Have you been over to Maureen's yet?" he asked her.

She stopped and looked blankly at him. "Excuse me?"

"Your friend Maureen," he prompted. "You said you were going to set her straight."

Noelle sighed. "Colby Brennan, meet Joy's twin sister, Grace."

His eyebrows shot up in surprise. "Twin?"

Grace nodded, friendly but definitely more reserved than her sister. "Identical. But we never wear the same clothes."

Colby shrugged helplessly. "I'm sorry. I didn't pay any attention to what Joy was wearing."

Noelle grinned at Grace. "Men rarely pay close attention to what women wear, but don't let that get out, or I'd lose three fourths of my customers."

Back at his office, Colby reflected, he'd been able to recall exactly what Noelle had been wearing, right down to the low-heeled pink shoes on her feet. He had even imagined what she was wearing beneath the suit. Lace, he thought. Lace and silk.

Grace pointed behind him. "Joy's over there."

He glanced over his shoulder and saw Joy chatting up his two friends in her charmingly natural flirtatious way. With a grin he looked back at Grace. "Sorry I mistook you, but I'm probably not the first person who's done it."

"Not by a long shot. Being mistaken for each other comes with the job description of being an identical twin."

"Well, it's nice to meet you, Grace. May I ask you

a few questions later? I'll be questioning your sister also."

"Sure. I'll be glad to help in any way. Just let me know." With a smile at Noelle she strolled off.

"Interesting girls," Colby said, returning his attention to Noelle.

"They're great," she said in an adamant tone that dared him to differ.

So much for easing the tension. "I'm not the bad guy here, Noelle. Try to remember that. I'm only trying to find out what happened."

She pressed a thumb and finger against her eyelids. "I'm sorry."

He closed his long fingers around her wrist and pulled her hand away from her face. "And stop apologizing to me."

She stared at him, his strong, warm touch paralyzing her thought processes. Thankfully, after a moment he released her hand. Instinctively she took a step backward. She would have increased the distance between them more if she thought she could do it without him noticing. "What do you want to know?"

He noticed, but he let it be. She was still within arm's reach. "Tell me about Joy and Grace. How long have they worked for you?"

"About a year. They're students at SMU. They work here for extra money and the discount I give them on their clothes, but I'm the one who makes out on the deal."

"Why's that?"

"They're a walking advertisement for me. Anything I put on them looks fabulous. On Saturdays they model clothes from my stock, and I literally sell the clothes right off their backs several times during the day. Plus, a lot of their friends come here because of the clothes they wear on campus."

"I've only seen you in what you have on today, but I would imagine you could wear a paper bag and look pretty fabulous yourself." Of course, he thought, he also had no doubt that she would look fabulous without any clothes, lying on his bed, her hair spread out over his pillow. . . . He burned just thinking about it.

As his touch had, the compliment threw her completely off guard. "Thank you." All at once self-conscious, she looked down at her hands. "Is that all you want to know?"

"No. Do the twins have any regular boyfriends?"

"Joy has a score of boyfriends. She believes it's more fun to play the field than to tie herself down to one boy."

"Do you agree with that theory?"

There was something in his tone that made her ask, "Are you talking about Joy or me now?"

"You."

She hesitated. "Is this a question related to the case?"

Hell no, he thought, but if it made her feel safer to think so . . . "Of course."

"Then yes, I do."

"So there's no one special in your life?"

"No. I go out with a number of men."

No one special was good, he thought, but he wasn't sure he liked the sound of "a number of men." There was safety in numbers, but at the same time . . . "And what about Grace?"

"Grace dates, but not anyone in particular and not as much as Joy. She's very serious about her studies."

"To your knowledge, have either of them had any trouble with anyone, a date, a friend?"

"No. They're very well liked. Joy has a way of turning down a boy and making him feel as if he's the luckiest guy in the world, and Grace is equally kind." She shook her head, upset that he seemed to be targeting the twins. "Look, you're totally wrong if you think they had anything to do with this. They don't need the money. They come from a wealthy family in Dallas. In fact, each has a trust fund, but they're responsible, hardworking girls who don't happen to feel that it's better if everything in life is handed to them. They're to be admired. And they're *not*, I repeat *not*, involved."

"I admire your loyalty, Noelle, but I have to check out everything. It's part of my job."

His job. She glanced over at the two police officers. "I heard them say something about you being with them. Were you a police officer?"

He nodded. "For seven years."

Officer Klein sauntered up, interrupting them, so that she had no way of knowing if Colby would have said anything more.

"We're almost through, Miss Durrell. We did manage to lift a few prints from the jewelry cases, so we're going to have to fingerprint you and your employees."

"I understand."

"I would have thought you would find more than a few prints," Colby said.

"Someone always cleans the cases right before we close each night," she explained.

Colby nodded. "Well, at least that'll make things a little easier. It should eliminate any customers."

Officer Klein looked at Noelle. "We'd like to fingerprint you and the two girls right now, if it's all right."

"No problem."

The next few minutes were taken up with the fingerprinting, and then, with a few quiet words to Colby, the two officers were gone. Noelle waited until the twins had washed the ink from their fingers, then went to the rest room to wash hers. When she came back, Colby was waiting for her, amid several racks of clothes that hadn't been put out yet.

"Yes?"

He silently cursed. The wariness was there again. It made him feel as awkward as a schoolboy, but it also challenged him. "I'd like to question Grace and Joy now, if you can spare them."

She shrugged. "If you feel you have to, but you're wasting your time."

"It's procedure, that's all. The questions are routine."

She tilted her head. "You sound just like a cop. Why did you leave the force?"

He didn't move, but it seemed to her as if he pulled back from her.

"There were several reasons," he said curtly. The puzzled expression on her face sent a pain shooting through his gut. Why hadn't he given her the standard answer he usually gave? Why did every word he said to her seem to take on such importance in his mind?

"I'm sorry," she murmured. "I shouldn't have asked."

He held up a hand. "Stop apologizing, Noelle. Nothing is your fault."

Her expression was as cool as ice. "The apology was simply an attempt at being polite." She turned on her heels and went back into the shop.

And he was left silently cursing at himself.

A short time later he was sitting at Noelle's desk in her office, winding up the questioning of Joy. "Have any of your friends ever expressed an unusual interest in the merchandise here in the store?"

With a little laugh Joy carelessly combed her fingers through her hair. When she dropped her hand to her lap, her hair slid back into place, a smooth, glistening sheet of white-blond. "Noelle Durrell's is the absolute coolest place in town to shop. My friends are green with envy that I get to work here. If Noelle would expand and carry some of the better lines of jeans, she'd double her business." She gave him a sly look. "By the way, Noelle looks great in jeans."

He smiled easily. "I'm sure she does." Joy was one of the most open people he had ever come across, and not one bit perturbed that her attempt to talk Noelle up to him was blatantly transparent. What she didn't know was that her efforts were totally unnecessary.

"Has anyone ever asked you if you had a key to the shop?"

"Nope."

"Have you noticed anyone strange hanging around the area lately?"

"No. Everyone is really nice around here, and the customers are all dolls."

He smiled. He had asked Grace the same questions and had received more or less the same answers. But Grace's answers were carefully and thoughtfully given, whereas Joy blurted out her thoughts. No subterfuge there.

"Have you had an argument with anyone, anyone at all, recently?"

"Nope. I get along with everyone, and I don't have a regular boyfriend." Her blue eyes held lights of laughter. "Of course, when I get to be as old as you, I'll probably want to start thinking about settling down."

His lips quirked. "Of course. That and look into cemetery plots. Okay, that's it for now, but keep thinking, and if you remember anything unusual that's happened over the last few weeks, give me a call."

"You bet." She grinned saucily. "Would you like me to send Noelle in now?"

He hesitated. "Yes, please, if she has time."

As he settled back in the chair, waiting for Noelle to appear, his pulses quickened in expectation of her arrival. He had known her for only a few hours, and already she dominated his thoughts. Amazing when he considered how little he knew about her. It was a situation he wanted to correct immediately. But in this instance there were two things that stood in the way of his getting what he wanted: that formidable guard she seemed to reserve exclusively for him, and the necessity of solving the burglary. Unfortunately he had a feeling that the former would be infinitely harder than the latter.

Her office was very organized, very feminine. Her desk was a mahogany Queen Anne; the desk set was blue-and-rose cloisonné. In one corner a small cut-crystal vase held pens and pencils. A bound leather calendar lay open on another corner. And he couldn't help but notice that quite a few dates had men's names written in beneath them, including one beneath the current date: *Gary—seven-thirty.*

Jealousy stabbed through him, pure, strong, and painful, and he was left shaking. He leaned his head against the leather back of the chair and closed his eyes for a moment, willing the emotion away. He couldn't remember ever feeling jealousy before. It was a revelation to him, and not a welcome one either.

He was thirty-seven. There had been women in his life, relationships. And more than once he had thought a relationship might develop into something serious. The fact that none had ever done so had never bothered him. But he was bothered now—in fact, much more than bothered. He was downright perturbed that after only a few hours Noelle had had such an effect on him.

It didn't seem right that after knowing her for only a short time he should care so fiercely about whether or not she saw someone named Gary tonight at seven-thirty. Or that she had seen Max last Wednesday night, or that she was going to see Bill Saturday night. She hadn't been kidding when she'd said she dated a number of men.

He needed to reassess his thinking about Noelle, get himself under control. It was damned uncomfortable to feel so strongly about her in such a short time. Especially when it appeared she didn't come close to returning the feeling.

Even though he still had his eyes shut, he knew the very second she entered the office because of her perfume. It was a light, faintly floral fragrance that carried with it a whisper of sensuality. He had noticed the scent before; it lingered around her, an enhancement of her own female scent, a device to drive sane thoughts from a man's formerly sane mind.

He opened his eyes and saw her standing before her desk, watching him.

"So, are you satisfied now that the girls had nothing to do with this?"

"Pretty much."

"You still have doubts?"

He watched the gold sparks flare in the depths of her brown eyes and had to admit he had given her a qualified answer merely to see them. It had been a capricious act on his part, something very rare with him. But it fit with her unusual effect on him.

"When a case has as few leads as this one seems to, you don't rule out anyone or anything."

"And that includes me?"

"No, it doesn't, but I would like to ask you some questions." He gestured to the chair he was sitting in. "Would you like to trade places?"

"I'm fine where I am." She suspected that if she took the chair behind her desk, he would choose to stand, which meant she would have to look up at him. She didn't need the psychological disadvantage. "I really don't have anything to add to what I said earlier."

"Sometimes we have information that we aren't aware that we have. I'd really appreciate it if you would think about it. Maybe you'll remember something. You have my office number, but I'll give you my home number too." He reached into the inside pocket of his jacket and produced a card from a slim wallet. On its back he wrote a number and handed it to her. "Don't hesitate to call if you remember anything at all. Something you might think is insignificant could prove to be a key piece of information."

She glanced at the card, then laid it on top of the calendar. "Is that all?"

His jaw flexed. He stood and rounded the desk. "Not quite."

The hard, dangerous light she had first noticed in his eyes this morning was back. "What is it?"

"Have dinner with me tonight."

Her breath caught in her throat. "Why?"

Damned good question. Hadn't he just decided that he needed to rearrange his thinking where she was concerned? "To discuss the break-in." She eyed him with the wariness he was growing to hate. It made him want to jerk her to him and kiss her until neither of them could stand—totally inappropriate behavior, but Lord how he wanted to do it!

"Have you found out anything?"

"Nothing new, but I thought if we talked, you might remember something. And I do have more questions." Questions regarding her private life that he hadn't yet been able to bring himself to ask because he was afraid of the answers. He couldn't remember the last thing that had frightened him. He hadn't even been frightened of a sharp, glistening knife wielded by a stone-cold killer in that dark alley. . . .

She glanced toward her calendar, then shook her head. "It probably wouldn't be a very productive meeting, but I can't anyway. I have plans for tonight."

Meeting? He had asked her to dinner, and she had called it a meeting? He supposed it was his own fault, the way he had presented the evening to her. And he shouldn't have asked her anyway. He, too, looked at the calendar. "You have a date?"

She didn't have a date, not in the strictest meaning of the word. Gary was an old friend who was going to come over and cook pasta for them, and then they were going to watch an old movie on television. But since Colby Brennan was the person asking her, she felt the need to tell a white lie. "Yes."

"With this Gary?" He poked his finger at the offending name marked on the calendar.

Her mouth dropped open. "You looked at my calendar?"

He didn't try to whitewash his snooping. "It was open, and your handwriting is easy to read."

She drew herself up to her full five-foot-five-inch height. "Get out, Mr. Brennan."

He closed the distance between them with a speed that took her by surprise.

"You're going to call me Colby before too very long."

His closeness brought heat rushing to her skin,

and a false arrogance to her response. "I see no reason why I should."

He lightly brushed a finger against her cheek. "Just chalk it up to my desire to hear you say my name, and be thankful that's the only desire I'm demanding be fulfilled for now." He walked to the door with only the barest unevenness showing in his gait. "I'll leave, but I'll be back. Oh, and have a nice rest of the day."

"Thank you," she said, cool on the outside, shaken on the inside. It felt as though he had burned her cheek, when in fact he had only lightly touched her. "I will."

And she'd have a nice evening too, she thought with defiance. Pasta and old movies with a good friend was one of her favorite ways to spend an evening.

So then why did she have a feeling that even Humphrey Bogart brooding over a glass of champagne in Rick's Place and a luminescent Ingrid Bergman asking Sam to "play it again" wouldn't be enough to take her mind off a green-eyed security-agency owner who had spoken of demanding that desire be fulfilled?

Three

Sottise hid his eyes beneath his paws and whimpered.

Mrs. Wharton, a robust woman with auburn hair, glanced at him, then returned her gaze to her reflection in the three-way mirror. "Noelle, Sottise doesn't like this particular necklace with this outfit, and I have to agree with him. What about the one you're wearing? I've been admiring it ever since I walked in. Quartz, isn't it? Is it the shop's or yours?"

"The shop's," Noelle said smoothly.

Just as she used the twins to model clothes, she often accessorized her own outfits from her stock to show her customers how an outfit could have a new look with a simple change of earrings, a belt, or a scarf. As sometimes happened with certain pieces, she had grown quite fond of the necklace and wasn't yet ready to part with it, but that didn't prevent her from suggesting it to Mrs. Wharton. She instinctively knew the necklace wouldn't look good on the woman. Mrs. Wharton needed something that provided more color near her face. Nevertheless she took off the quartz necklace and put it on Mrs. Wharton.

She checked her customer's image in the mirror, then met her eyes. Sottise's whimpering grew louder. And both women shook their heads.

"Let's try another one," Noelle said. "I've just remembered a copper necklace that should go beautifully with your outfit and your auburn hair. All *right*, Sottise, that's enough."

Noelle replaced the quartz necklace around her own neck and fished a copper necklace with blue stones from a case. The minute she hooked the necklace around Mrs. Wharton's neck, she knew it was the right look for the new outfit the woman had worn to the shop. So did Sottise. His ears lifted, and he barked approvingly.

Sottise fancied himself a fashion arbiter. As each woman came out from the dressing room in a new outfit or tried on an accessory, it was his practice to pass judgment. Noelle had tried to break him of the habit, but the regular customers who had caught on to his ways loved his criticism, and, surprisingly, most of the time he was right.

With a big smile Mrs. Wharton patted the necklace. "This is the one."

"Wonderful. I'll wrap it up for you."

Automatically she checked to see if Grace needed any help; as usual the girl was doing a superb job. Joy had left for her afternoon classes, but Noelle and Grace were having no trouble handling the flow of traffic that had developed since they reopened at around two o'clock. Over the past year Grace had become expert at keeping track of which lady was in each dressing room and what her needs were.

As Noelle was writing up the necklace, thunder

rumbled overhead, and big splatters of rain hit the windows.

Grace walked by, her outstretched arms laden with dresses for the lady in dressing room 2. "Where did that rain come from? The last time I looked outside, the sun was shining."

Noelle glanced out the window, then with a frown returned to the task of completing the sales transaction. "I don't know. It's an odd day. Unpredictable. Things are happening that shouldn't."

"You mean the burglary?"

"That and other things." Mostly her reaction to Colby Brennan. "Here you are, Mrs. Wharton," she said, handing her a glossy red-and-white-striped bag containing the necklace. "I know you're going to be happy with your selection."

Mrs. Wharton beamed. "I know I am, too, and thank you so much. Bye, Sottise."

Sottise wagged his tail and gave her a cheery good-bye bark.

Noelle crossed the floor to check on the progress of a lady who was sorting through a rack of items on sale, but turned back when she heard the phone ring. She grabbed up the closest phone, the one on the gracefully lined cherrywood desk where she and the girls sat to write up purchases. "Noelle Durrell."

"Miss Durrell, this is Mort Seager."

Mort Seager was the foreman of the crew she had hired to paint her house, and she knew why he was calling before she asked. "Yes?"

"I'm afraid we're going to have to knock off painting a few hours earlier than we had planned because of the rain."

Noelle checked her watch. Because of the extra hours of light daylight saving time gave, the painters had been scheduled to work at least three more hours. "Don't worry about it. I understand. Hopefully you can get in a full day tomorrow."

"I hope so, too, but I'm not counting on it. A new weather report is calling for more rain tomorrow. This is going to play havoc with my schedule."

Hers too, she thought gloomily. She had hoped to have the house completed and the painters gone by the weekend. "Let's be optimistic. Didn't the weatherman call for sun today? When it comes right down to it, he's guessing along with the rest of us."

"Well, I sure hope he's wrong this time."

"Me too. I'll talk to you in the morning."

She hung up the phone and turned, and as she did, the quartz necklace slid from her neck. "Dammit," she exclaimed, and caught it in her hands. Holding it up, she examined it and saw that the clasp was broken. "Great. First the burglary, then the rain, and now this. This simply isn't my day. I'd love to know what my horoscope said."

"Were you talking to me?" Grace asked, passing by.

"No, just myself. It's probably a bad sign, but then what else is new?"

Grace patted her on the back. "Don't worry. The day's almost over. What else can happen?"

She grinned. "You're absolutely right, and I don't know why I'm complaining. I've got an evening with Gary, pasta, and Humphrey Bogart to look forward to. What could be better than that?" An image of Colby Brennan flashed into her head.

With a scowl that had nothing to do with the rain or the broken clasp, she headed toward her office at the back of the store and deposited the necklace in her purse. She shouldn't be surprised about the clasp. Kenneth Kaye himself had been in touch with her about defective workmanship on the clasps of some of his pieces. He'd urged her to return the shipment, but after checking the stock she'd declined. An honorable businessman. She liked that. No problem. Repaired, the necklace would be as good as new and ready for sale, but the trick would be finding the time to take it to the jeweler.

Noelle's hours for the shop were ten to six, but invariably there were still customers in the store at closing time. She never complained, though. The success of her store had been built on personalized service, and she was never happier than when she was matching the right person with the right wardrobe.

Tonight, though, perhaps because of the rain, the customers had thinned out early, until at five-thirty there was only one left, and Grace in her quiet, competent way was taking care of her.

Fifteen minutes later Colby walked in, and both Grace and the customer turned to look at him. Noelle did too. He was hard *not* to look at. Even though the label of his jeans would no doubt be more common to a rodeo than a fashion mall, the cut of his sports coat told her it wasn't off the rack. And he hadn't gotten his boots at any discount store. She didn't have to ask to know that he had been born and raised in Texas. No one but a Texan could quite get the blend right. It was a casual yet expensive look that could go from a boardroom to a stockyard with equal aplomb. And on Colby Brennan the look was devastatingly sexual and forcefully masculine.

She was extremely annoyed. She'd been trying to get him out of her mind all afternoon, and here he was, larger than life and sexier than any man had a right to be.

"I didn't expect to see you again today," she said curtly when he crossed to her.

He eyed her appraisingly, taking in the signs of strain in her face. He hated having to add to that strain, but the truth was, he wouldn't have been able to keep away from her, no matter what. "You mean you were *hoping* you wouldn't."

"I said what I meant, Mr. Brennan."

A smile played around his lips, softening his hard face. "You're determined not to say my name, aren't you?"

His smile was as tempting as a flame to a moth, but she wasn't about to allow herself to self-destruct. She threw a quick glance over her shoulder and saw that Grace was writing up a purchase for their last customer. "I'm about to close for the day. Why are you here?"

"Cool," he murmured. "Too cool actually, but I'll leave it for now. I'm here to ask you to change your mind and have dinner with me tonight."

"I've already told you I have plans."

"Change them, Noelle. You and I need to talk."

"About what?"

"Anything you'd like to talk about, but first we need to talk about the break-in."

"Okay, let's talk here. I've already given you all the information I have, so I know it won't take long."

"Wrong. It will take a while. And I'm hungry."

"You're . . . ?" She didn't know how he did it, but he could slip under her skin and nettle her until complete incoherence was a definite possibility.

"Noelle, I have some new information that I'm taking very seriously, and you should too."

"How *can* I when you won't tell me what it is?"

"We seem to be going around in circles here," he said, gently pointing out the obvious, "but I'll say it again. I will tell you at dinner. Now call Gary and cancel."

Color rushed up beneath her skin. Her evening with Gary and Humphrey Bogart promised to be pleasant and tranquil. An evening with Colby Brennan, no matter how short and businesslike, would offer the exact opposite. But she needed to be fair.

Even though he had a huge vested interest in figuring out who had gotten past his security system, he was also working on *her* behalf. She should be grateful, not antagonistic. And, she reasoned, the sooner the matter of the break-in was settled, the sooner Colby Brennan would be out of her life for good. In a month or two she would quietly switch to another security company. The plan made her feel better. And worse. "All right. Stay here, and I'll go call Gary. Oh, and I'll have to take Sottise to the house first."

Grace had just showed the customer to the door when she overheard Noelle. "If it will help, I can take him home with me. He can spend the night."

She hesitated. Since Joy and Grace had come to work for her, they kept Sottise for her on those rare occasions when she had to be out of town overnight. She much preferred him staying with them than having to board him. But there really wasn't any reason for them to keep him tonight. "Thanks, Grace, but it won't take me that long to drop him off at home."

"Please," Grace said with a pleading smile. "You know Joy and I love it when he spends the night with us. Joy has a date tonight, but I have to stay up late studying. I'd love to have him as company."

Torn, Noelle glanced at Sottise. Somehow knowing he was being talked about, he was gazing up at them, energetically wagging his tail. The house always felt so empty when he wasn't there, but—

"For heaven's sake," Colby said, impatience blatant in his tone, "you're talking about a *dog*, not a child. What does it matter where he spends the night?"

Grace's expression held pity. "You don't have a pet, do you?"

He threw up his hands. Noelle hid a laugh. "You can have Sottise for the night, Grace. Take his pillow and blanket, and—oh, do you still have some of his food left over from his last visit?"

"Sure do."

"Great. And thank you."

Insisting on driving her own car, Noelle followed Colby's dark green Jaguar to a small Mexican restaurant. The ambience was strictly south of the border, with colored lights strung from beam to beam and sombreros vying with large paper flowers for wall space.

Noelle noticed the waitress, a nice-looking straw-berry blonde who was over by the bar, send a longing glance Colby's way. He missed the glance entire-ly, because he was looking at her. Or maybe, she thought, vexed, he was just used to longing glances from women. "Do you come here often?"

He took a healthy swallow of beer. "I come here a couple of times a week. The food's great, isn't it?"

She nodded appreciatively and reached for the container of hot sauce. "I have to admit it is."

"Go easy on that sauce. It's a five-alarm variety."

"I'm used to spicy foods." She forked a portion of chicken enchilada covered with the sauce into her mouth, and then immediately reached for her glass of water. When she could talk again, she gasped, "You weren't kidding, were you?"

"I'd never kid about hot sauce. This place has the best in town."

"And the *hottest*." Noelle waved a hand in front of her face in a futile attempt to cool herself off. "Next time I have a cold, I'll come here. This hot sauce really opens up your head."

"Even if you don't have a cold."

She laughed, and he was satisfied. He could have taken her to any place in Dallas, but he had brought her here not only because it was one of his favorite places to eat, but also because it had a casual, laid-back atmosphere, some of which he was hoping would rub off on her. He had stopped kidding him-self. The evening was only partially business. The rest of it would be an attempt to get to know her better.

She watched him run a tortilla through the hot sauce and then nonchalantly pop it into his mouth. "You must have a cast-iron stomach."

He grinned. "Pretty much. It comes from years of being a bachelor, not to mention a cop. When you're on stakeout, the mainstay of your diet is fast food." His voice softened. "Hey, listen, I'm sorry I was so short with you earlier today when you asked me why I left the force."

"Don't worry about it. I wasn't offended." To show that she wasn't, she sipped more water and casually glanced around the restaurant. The place was packed, but they were sitting in a large corner booth, secluded and private. She looked back at him to see his dark green eyes contemplating her with an unreadable expression.

"Do you still want to know?"

She did and she didn't. She was intensely curious about him, but with knowledge came familiarity, something she'd taken about two seconds to decide against when she had first met him. To her complete dismay, she found herself choosing a middle ground. "If you'd like to tell me."

"I was wounded, a knife into my leg. It wasn't a big thing, but I was left with a slight disability, enough to have kept me off the streets and put me behind a desk full time. The police force meant a great deal to me, but in the end I decided I could help people in other ways, without the rules and restrictions that police have to work with."

Now that she knew, she wished that she didn't.

She was trying to keep their relationship on a business level, and he had just told her something extremely personal. And she had issued him an invitation to do so. Oh, maybe it hadn't been gilt-edged, but it had been an invitation nevertheless. And it scared her. She glanced at her watch, trying to remember what time *Casablanca* had been scheduled to air.

She couldn't remember—her mind was too scrambled. She shoved her plate away from her and folded her hands on the table. "Okay, Mr. Brennan, I know you didn't bring me here simply to have my taste buds seared to a crisp. What is this new information?"

His eyebrows rose, and incredibly his eyes darkened. "Changing the subject, are we?"

"Your new information was supposed to *be* the subject."

His eyes went frosty. "What's the matter? Does the idea of a disabled man bother you?"

"*Disabled? You?*" She couldn't have been more astonished. "What are you doing?" she asked, completely baffled at his attitude. "Fishing for compliments?"

"I asked you a simple question. Answer it."

She was too shocked even to notice he had given her an order. "*No,* I'm not bothered by the idea of a disabled man, but at the moment I don't see one around, so I can't really prove that statement." The frost remained in his eyes, and suddenly it all came clear to her. He was self-conscious about that almost imperceptible unevenness of his gait that she had noticed this morning.

Men! Her mind silently screamed the word. They were so damned macho, so concerned with their egos and what they perceived as their masculinity. . . .

Her heart went out to him. His wound might not have been "a big deal," but it had taken him from a job that he had obviously loved. Granted, he had found another, equally satisfying career—she knew that because of the seriousness with which he was taking the break-in of her shop—but he saw his slight limp as an imperfection.

Without thinking about the repercussions, she reached for the one thing she thought might soothe him, something he had been wanting. She called him by his name. "Stop feeling sorry for yourself, Colby. You have no reason."

Something flickered in his eyes, then he plowed his hands through his hair with a sound of disgust. "You're absolutely right. I don't know what got into me."

But he *did* know. It was Noelle and her importance to him. Right after the stabbing, the doctors had used the word "disabled"; so had the police department. But he had never let himself think in those terms. He had simply gone to work and pushed himself to his absolute limit night and day until he had regained the use of his leg. And now a dark-eyed, dark-haired, slender beauty had come along and made him have doubts about himself.

Stupid, stupid, stupid.

But she had called him by his name.

"You called me Colby."

Because she was so relieved that the frost had left

his eyes, she smiled. "You told me I would before too very long, and something tells me you get your way a lot."

"Yeah, I do." But with her he hadn't been sure. He still wasn't. "I'm sorry. If it's any consolation, that outburst was as much a surprise to me as it was to you."

She shrugged, uncomfortable with the intimacy of the moment and wanting it to pass. "Maybe it's the day. It's been strange, totally unpredictable."

He looked intently at her. "Yeah, I know what you mean."

"The good news is, it's about to be over."

He wasn't sure he regarded that as good news. It was a reminder that he was going to have only a short time with her tonight.

"So what is it that we need to talk about?"

And in a wink they were back to business. He sighed, resigned to the fact that it had to be done. "I know how my system was bypassed. One of my men figured it out this afternoon."

"Well, that's good, isn't it? That's what you wanted to know."

He took his time answering her. The trick was to give her enough information so that she would understand why she needed to cooperate with him, but not enough to panic her. "You're right. It's what I wanted to know, but in finding out I've been left with more questions."

"I'm afraid I don't understand."

"I've found out how, but now more than ever I need to know why and who. You see, the system was bypassed in such a way that the signal that goes from your store to my control center wasn't disrupted. That's why on my end they didn't realize anything was wrong. And they did it with a device that they shouldn't have been able to get their hands on. It's high-high tech. Beyond state-of-the-art."

She shrugged. "So? People who operate outside the law, and even some who don't, seem to be able to purchase all sorts of things they shouldn't. After all, aren't fully automatic weapons supposed to be banned? According to the newspapers, you can buy one on practically any street corner in the city."

He shook his head. "This device is too extraordinary to be purchased on a street corner or even on the black market. No, whoever broke into your store was a pro, Noelle."

The hairs on the back of her neck stood on end. "But that doesn't make sense."

His expression was grim. "No, it doesn't, does it? Unless there's something you haven't told me."

"Like what?" she snapped sarcastically. "Like the fact that I'm selling cocaine from the back room? Ooops. Sorry. I meant to mention that, I really did."

He reached over and closed his hand over hers. "Relax."

"How? You just accused me of keeping important information from you and the police."

He shook his head. "I didn't mean it the way it came out. What I meant was that you may know something you're not even aware that you know."

"That's impossible." She jerked her hand away.

"Not really. Every day we see and hear things that go into our subconscious. Sometimes they stay there. Sometimes they can govern our actions without our even knowing it. Other times an event will act as a trigger, and the memory will come out."

She shook her head, bewildered. "The break-in has to be a mistake, Colby. It has to be. It's the only explanation."

She had called him Colby again and hadn't even realized it. The pleasure he felt was all out of proportion. "Maybe you're right. It could also be someone after me."

"*You?*"

He nodded coolly. "It's a theory I have to consider. Your shop could have been a test run for something more important."

"Test run?"

"My organization protects a chain of jewelry stores and a bank."

"Good Lord." Stunned at the implications, she sat back in the booth.

He smiled thinly. "So you see, you could be absolutely right in thinking your place wasn't really meant to be robbed, but for an entirely different reason. And the jewelry and money could have been taken to throw us off."

Her eyes were wide with concern. "Then what are you doing here? Why aren't you working on that possibility?"

"I already have been. All afternoon. And the proper precautions are being taken. But in any case we need to explore a few areas of your life, just to make sure all the bases are covered."

"What areas?"

One brow arched. "That's very impressive, Noelle, that guard you have. But it's not needed with me."

She strongly disagreed, but for reasons he knew nothing about. "What do you want to know?"

"Do you have any enemies?"

She looked at him calmly. "I don't know what kind of life you lead or what kind of people you deal with, but I don't know a soul who would want to hurt me." Not even Ed, though heaven knew they had fought hard enough when they had been together. "Can you say the same?"

"No, but then it wasn't my store that was burglarized, was it?"

The waitress came sashaying over and positioned herself so that Noelle's view of Colby was partially blocked.

"Do you want anything else, Colby, honey?"

"No, thanks." He shifted so that he could meet Noelle's eyes. "How about you? Coffee?" She shook her head. "That'll be it, Sandy."

She laid the bill down on the table. "See you soon."

He nodded and, as soon as the waitress left, went back to his questions. "Let's assume that it wasn't someone who wanted to scare you or hurt you. We need to look at the possibility that there was something in your store someone wanted."

The waitress, Sandy, hadn't made the slightest impression on him, Noelle realized. He hadn't even noticed her obvious crush on him. She felt a surge of pity for the girl.

"Noelle?"

"What? Oh, we've already been over this. Clothes and costume jewelry. That's what I carry."

"There's got to be something else."

"There's not."

He leaned forward. "Noelle, I don't want to scare you, but at the moment we're exploring the theory that it was your store he was after, and you need to know that whoever did it is so smart and has so much technology at his disposal that he could have gone through your shop like a knife through butter."

She looked at him blankly. "What are you getting at? He *did* get into my shop without you knowing about it."

"And once he was in, he was pretty damned messy, wasn't he? You see? He has the ability to have gotten in and out without you even knowing except for the lock on the back door. But mannequins were knocked over, clothes were on the floor, your jewelry displays were messed up. It was as if what he was looking for wasn't where he thought it would be."

"*Or*," she said triumphantly, "he discovered he was at the wrong place."

"And so he took twenty-five dollars, three pairs of gold earrings, and a couple of pieces of costume jewelry?"

"Why not? Once he was in, he probably figured he should get something for his trouble."

He shook his head. "I'm not ready to buy that theory quite yet."

She made a sound of frustration. "You are *so* stubborn."

"Yes, I am. And thorough. It's my job."

And that's all this was to him, she reminded herself forcefully. A job. No matter how much her pulses might race when he smiled at her, she had to remember that she was just a job to him. She glanced at her watch. "Are we through?"

"Why? Is Gary waiting for you?"

"I broke the date. Remember?"

He remembered. He hadn't been able to stand the thought of her being with another man tonight. And even though she was with him now, jealousy still ate at him. He didn't know what her relationship was with this Gary. Or with the Bill she was scheduled to see on Saturday. "Does he have a key to your store?"

"No."

"Does Bill?"

Her eyes widened. "You read my entire calendar, didn't you? You're completely unscrupulous."

"I'm whatever it takes, Noelle."

"That's it! I'm out of here."

She slid across the padded bench, but his fingers closed around her wrist in a steellike band, and his eyes were hard as he looked at her.

"Wait until I pay the check, and then I'll follow you home."

"I can make my own way home."

"I never said you couldn't, but I'm going to follow you home and wait until you're safely inside."

"You are so *damned* stubborn."

With a grin he released her hand to throw several bills onto the table. "Don't forget unscrupulous."

The windshield wipers swiped back and forth, clearing the rain from Noelle's windshield as she drove down the quiet, tree-lined street where she lived. She'd chosen the neighborhood because it was only ten minutes from her shop, but also because she had fallen in love with the bungalow built in the thirties that she had bought two years ago.

Now, approaching her house, she glanced into her rearview mirror. The green Jaguar was no more than three car lengths behind her. The man was impossible. She hadn't been able to stop him following her home, but she had no intention of inviting him in.

She turned into her driveway and parked. Normally in bad weather she would continue down the driveway to the back of the house and the detached garage, but tonight she didn't feel like wrestling with the heavy door. A garage-door opener was next on her list of things to purchase.

She dashed for the house and made it up onto the large covered porch without getting too wet. She inserted the key into the door and pushed it open, but right before she went in, she glanced over her shoulder. The Jaguar was idling at the curb, and Colby had rolled down the window so that he could see her. She waved at him. "Good night."

"Good night."

The sound of his voice reached her, soft as the rain, seductive as the darkness. And for one overwhelming moment she almost gave in and called to him to come in. Fortunately good sense won out. She went into the house and switched on the lights.

Then she screamed.

Four

Colby moved so fast, he made a series of actions look like one smooth movement. Within moments he was racing up to the porch, his gun drawn. He was just in time to catch Noelle with his free hand as she blindly bolted from the house.

"What's the matter?" he asked roughly, glancing at her to make sure she was all right, then looking over her shoulder. The part of the room he could see had been ransacked.

"My house," she gasped. "My house . . ."

He didn't have to see the blank expression in her eyes to know that she was in shock. He bent so that his gaze was level with hers and willed her to focus. "Noelle," he said, his tone urgent and firm, "go to my car and lock yourself in."

"My house . . ." Her tone carried faint censure, indicating she thought he didn't understand what she was saying.

"Noelle, listen to me. Go to my car and use the phone to call the police. I need to check inside. There's a chance someone might still be in there."

Her eyes narrowed slightly on him, the first sign he had that she was coming out of shock.

"Wait for the police," she said very clearly.

"You forget, I used to be a policeman." He turned her and with a gentle push headed her toward the porch steps. "*Go.*" Without waiting to see if she did, he entered the house, his gun raised.

Efficiently, methodically, he checked every room. When he finished searching, he swore loud and hard. He would have loved to have gotten his hands on the bastard who had been there. It looked as if Noelle's house had been turned upside down and shaken. Furniture was overturned, pictures had been stripped from the walls, books and knick-knacks had been thrown to the floor. Either the crook who had done this was the clumsiest person alive, or this was no ordinary burglary. He was betting on the latter.

He tucked his pistol into his belt at his back beneath his jacket and headed outside. Noelle was there, her arms clasped tightly around herself.

"I called the police," she said dully.

"You should have stayed in the car."

"I couldn't. It's my house."

He decided against arguing with her. If someone had still been on the premises, she could have put herself in danger by coming back up on the porch. *Then* he would have argued with her. Not now, though. He understood what she was going through; he had seen it too many times when he'd been on the force.

Someone had violated her home, a place, if she was like most people, where she felt safest. A stranger had touched her belongings, her treasures, that which she kept most private. This morning she had reacted in anger when she found that her store had been broken into, but a home was far more personal than a place of business. Invading a person's home was in some ways the equivalent of attacking the person.

He grasped her shoulders and gave a slight experimental tug. With a shudder she went into his arms and buried her face against his chest.

"It's going to be all right," he murmured, his mouth against her hair.

His arms felt like an island of sanity and security to her, and she didn't question the feeling. She couldn't. Quite simply she needed too badly the respite he was giving her.

His hands moved reassuringly up and down her back, driving away the chill that had lodged inside her. Funny, she thought, detached and remote, but she would never have guessed he would be capable of such gentleness.

She made a conscious decision. While still enclosed within the haven of his arms, she would ask the question she had been putting off. "Does the rest of my house look like the living room?"

"Yes." He felt the tremor that raced through her and held her tighter. Rage at the unknown perpetrator threatened to choke him, but he kept his voice even. "You don't have to go in there until you're ready."

"What's wrong with the world?" she asked, fighting back the nausea that had been threatening ever since she first saw her living room. "Why would anyone feel as if they have the right to break into someone else's home and tear it apart?"

She sounded like a bewildered, hurt child, he thought grimly, who had just been shown a totally new part of life she had never known existed and couldn't begin to comprehend it. He, on the other hand, knew a dark underside of life that made what had happened to her house look like a day at the beach. His gut knotted as his rage grew. With everything that was in him he wished he could have spared her her new knowledge.

"I don't know, Noelle. I suppose there are as many reasons as there are people." He leaned away from her, and with a knuckle beneath her chin gently lifted her face so that he could see her eyes. And he hated what he saw—fear, confusion, tears. For her sake he forced a grin. "If anyone ever figures out the solution, they could walk away with the Nobel Peace Prize."

"Right," she murmured.

The moments she was held in his arms had given her a chance to regain some of her strength, but now it was time to stand on her own once again. She pulled away from him and swiped at a stray tear. "And win *my* everlasting gratitude." She attempted a small laugh, but the intended laugh came out sounding like a sob. "What do you think the odds are of a person getting robbed twice in one day?"

He lightly brushed a hand over her hair. "I imagine they're pretty high. It must be your lucky day."

This time she did laugh. "Oh, is *that* what it is? *Luck?* I've been wondering."

A police car pulled to the curb behind Colby's car, and two men in uniform got out. They reached the porch and made their introductions.

Quickly and concisely Colby told them everything he knew, including something he hadn't told Noelle yet. "There's a small half-circle cut in one of the bedroom windows right above the lock. The screen is off, and the window is raised. I closed it because of the rain, but I was careful. If there are any prints, I didn't smudge them."

The officer who was writing down the details in his notebook nodded. "Sounds exactly like the other houses that were hit in the neighborhood tonight."

"There were other houses burglarized around here tonight?" Noelle asked in surprise.

"So far we've gotten four other calls. Two on this block and two directly behind you. Same thing. The owners were at work, and the entry was made through a back window."

The other officer shrugged. "It's not unusual for it to happen like that. It's a crook's version of one-stop shopping."

The policeman with the notebook made a sound of agreement. "It's a sort of while-I'm-in-the-neighborhood mentality."

"Were the other houses tossed like hers?" Colby asked.

The officer craned his neck and glanced around the door. "Pretty much." He looked back at Noelle. "Any idea yet what was taken?"

She shook her head. "I haven't even looked in there yet."

"Well, I don't want to ruin your day, but if it's like the others, your TV, stereo, VCR, and home computer, if you have one, will be gone."

She smiled ruefully. "Officer, you'd have to work

awfully hard to make my day any worse than it's already been. The dress shop that I own was burglarized this morning."

His eyebrows shot up. "*Really?* Do they have any idea who did it?"

"None."

He bent his head to jot something down in his notebook. Watching, Colby knew the officer was taking note of the two break-ins, but that chances were, unless a big fat arrow turned up, tying the two together or pointing to the person who'd done both of them, the two break-ins would be chalked up to coincidence.

"Someone from Physical Evidence will be out in the morning to dust that window," the first officer said, "but other than that, I don't see much point in asking you not to touch anything. You'll probably want to start straightening up. Also, this will be assigned to an investigator. He'll probably be in touch tomorrow too."

She exhaled wearily. "I know the drill. Thanks."

"Sure." With a nod he left with his partner.

She glanced up at Colby. "If my own little personal crime wave continues, I'll end up meeting the entire police force."

"Your sense of humor's coming back. That's a good sign."

Her smile was sad. "You're mistaking desperation for a sense of humor." Resigned to what she had to do, she eyed the front door, which was standing open. "I guess there's no putting it off."

"As a matter of fact, you can put it off as long as you like. You don't even have to go in there tonight if you don't want to."

She looked at him, remembering how she had gone into his arms. As uncharacteristic as that act had been for her, she was unable to regret those moments. "Thank you for following me home, Colby. I don't know what I would have done if I'd been alone—" Her voice broke.

He took a step closer to her. All his protective instincts were keen. "It's okay, Noelle. You're not alone."

No, thanks to him, she wasn't. Life was certainly strange. This morning she had been angry with him, tonight she had turned to him for comfort. And yesterday she hadn't even known him. "I'm really glad I didn't bring Sottise home," she said with a sudden thought. "What if he'd been here when the person broke in? He might have been hurt."

"To hell with the dog. What if *you'd* come home and walked in while the burglary was going down? You might have been more than just hurt." He didn't think it was possible for her to go any paler, but she did. He muttered an oath. "I'm sorry, Noelle. I didn't mean to frighten you."

"Don't worry about it. You're right. But I'm still glad Sottise wasn't here. And if I delay this any longer, I'll never go inside." Straightening, she turned and went into the house.

She walked slowly through the rooms, dimly grateful that Colby was right behind her. It was an effort, but she tried to block out the distress she felt at seeing her belongings turned topsy-turvy and concentrate on what might be missing.

She had used all her spare time in the last two years to renovate and decorate the little house. She had spent endless hours at flea markets, searching through stall after stall of odd-looking, broken-down furniture to find exactly the right pieces with which to furnish her home.

Now the buffet she had spent hours refinishing looked skeletal with all its drawers out and strewn about the room. The antique quilt she had thought so special had been pulled from the wall where she had hung it and tossed in a pile, without respect for the fragility of the cloth or the tiny stitching some long-ago hand had made. Pottery discovered one piece at a time by digging through countless barrels and bins lay broken.

Still, she held up pretty well until she reached her bedroom.

But the sight there stunned her. Her closet had been emptied, and all her clothes had been thrown on the floor. Her lingerie was spilled from its drawers. Even the mattress had been stripped from the bed and was half lying on the floor.

"It looks like two countries went to war," she murmured numbly.

Colby didn't answer her, because there was no answer. What had been done to her house was almost without reason. He'd really like to think the explanation was a couple of kids who had been looking for drug money. He'd like to, but unease nagged at him, an unease so pervasive, all he could think about was getting her away from there.

In the midst of the jumble, she spied an ornately decorated silver-backed hand mirror on the floor. She dropped to her knees and picked it up. Shards of the broken glass reflected a shattered image of her face. "Oh, no . . ." She quickly knelt to find the missing pieces, running her hands beneath brightly colored scarves and discarded jewelry.

From a distance, almost as if she were in a tunnel, she heard Colby's deep voice. "Noelle, you'll cut yourself."

Strong hands clasped her shoulders, and she was drawn to her feet. She swayed, then felt herself pulled back against him. "This was my grandmother's," she said, gazing down at the mirror. "She died six years ago. I still miss her."

"I'm sorry, Noelle."

"You know, I'm going to have to wash everything. The bedding, my clothes . . . even the walls. I want to sterilize everything he touched."

"Tomorrow. Or next week. But not tonight. Tonight, I want you to pack a few things and come home with me."

Hours before, she would have snapped his head off for even suggesting such a thing, but now she only shook her head. "No."

He gently but firmly turned her to face him. "*Yes.* You can't stay here, and even if you could, I wouldn't want you to be alone."

She had to admit the idea of being alone tonight was less than appealing to her, but resisting was automatic. "I've lived by myself a long time. I'll be all right."

"Sweet heaven, Noelle, look at this place." He swept a hand around the room. "There's no way you're going to be able to sleep here with things in this condition, and it would take you half the night even to make a dent in it."

Maybe he was right, she thought, scanning the disorder, but she couldn't be sure. She was finding it hard to put thoughts together. "I can go to a hotel."

"You'd still be alone," he pointed out, watching her closely. He was trying his level best to be considerate of her feelings, knowing that under normal circumstances the last thing she would want would be to spend the night at his house. On the other hand, he had an unalterable need to have her under the protection of his own roof. "If you don't like the idea of coming back to my house, what about the twins? Could you stay with them for the night?"

"They have a small apartment. I'd be putting them to a lot of trouble."

"I don't think they'd mind."

She bent her head and looked at the mirror again. "You're probably right, but I'm not sure." Her expression turned puzzled. "I don't know what's wrong with me, but I seem to be having trouble thinking straight."

His jaw firmed, and his attempt at being considerate ended. "You've had a shock, that's what's wrong with you. And you don't have to think. You're coming home with me. Now do you want to make a guess where an overnight bag would be, or do you just want to use a paper bag?"

Noelle gazed around her, somewhat bemused. She was in Colby's home, a loft located on the sixth floor of a six-story renovated warehouse on the edge of downtown Dallas. The details of exactly how he had gotten her to agree to come with him were a little fuzzy to her. But she remembered sitting beside him in his Jaguar, meek as a lamb, as he drove her through the rain-soaked streets.

Well, why not? she thought wearily. Why not simply accept her presence in his loft as part and parcel of this curious day? Nothing else made sense. Why should this? Maybe she would feel differently tomorrow, but she couldn't be bothered with worrying now. . . .

She was sitting on a black, glove-leather sofa, exactly where Colby had left her. She wasn't sure how long she had been there, but she was comfortable, and that was enough for the present.

Outside, the rain continued, pattering against the industrial floor-to-ceiling windows with a steady rhythm, blurring the panoramic view of downtown Dallas so that the lights appeared to shimmer.

Plush Oriental rugs rested atop a sealed concrete floor and defined the vast space of the main living area. Directly in front of her a glistening block of polished black granite served as a cocktail table. Beyond the living area she could see Colby in a kitchen that looked to be both an architectural statement and an extremely efficient place to prepare meals. And everywhere there were tall, slender cream-colored candles rising from all shapes and sizes of crystal candle holders.

Raw, massive, stark, sensual—the place suited him, she decided.

He crossed to her, placing a tray down on the marble table. "I made hot tea," he said, dropping down beside her. "And I put sugar in it."

"I don't take sugar in my tea."

Her voice was so soft, he had to bend toward her to hear her. "Drink it with sugar tonight. For me."

As brain-dead as she currently was, she still knew that there were probably scores of women who would love to do anything he asked. If only for the principle of it, she thought about telling him no, but quickly decided it would be too much effort. She took the cup he offered her and sipped. The sweet, hot liquid curled through her, warming her.

He smiled that charming smile she had first seen in her store this morning. "For a second there, I thought you wouldn't do it."

She didn't want to be jarred out of the cushioned world where she had retreated, but his smile, along with the tea, was a powerful draw. "You underestimate your powers of persuasion."

"More like I underestimated how tired you are."

"I *am* tired." She nodded toward a forest of candles populating the top of a sleek credenza. "Does your sister hold stock in a candle company?"

He chuckled, a sound that warmed her even more than the tea. Against her wishes, she was definitely beginning to feel again.

"In addition to thinking my decor needed a feminine touch, she thought they would come in handy in case of a power outage."

"Or a romantic evening."

"Or a romantic evening," he agreed, an image instantly springing to his mind of how Noelle would look wearing nothing but candlelight.

She sipped her tea. "You have quite a place here. Unusual."

"It's been very practical. I bought the building

with the idea of an investment, and it's paid off. When I first moved in I was the only person living here, and until the renovations were completed, the accommodations were pretty rough. But now I have a building full of good tenants, and a great view no matter what window I look out."

"I renovated my house too. Of course, my house is so much smaller. . . ."

And homier, he thought. As he had walked through her house with her, he had been able to imagine what it had looked like before it had been torn apart. And his rage had been fed.

She shouldn't have mentioned her home, she thought. Like a camera, her mind had taken pictures of the rooms of her house, and she couldn't get those pictures out of her mind.

"You had a gun, didn't you?"

"I didn't think you saw it, but yes. I have a license to carry a concealed weapon. I have several, and I keep one under the seat of my car." He shrugged. "Habit, I guess, but I'm sorry if I frightened you."

"*You* didn't." She put down the cup of half-drunk tea. "You were a good police officer, weren't you?"

"What makes you say that?"

"I can tell."

"I guess I was fair."

"My bet is you couldn't be just fair at anything."

One brow raised. "Is that a compliment, Noelle?"

"I guess it is."

He grinned. "I'll take it. It's probably the last one I'll get from you."

She rubbed her forehead.

"Does your head hurt?"

She had to think about his question before she could decide on her answer. "No. I guess I'm really tired."

He took her hand. "Come on, I'll put you to bed."

"I'm not *that* tired. I can put myself to bed."

He drew her to her feet, pleased with the sign of spirit. "Then I'll show you to the bedroom."

Double doors set between two giant support columns led to the bedroom—a *spectacular* bedroom that almost didn't seem real to Noelle.

A wall of windows curved upward from the floor and didn't stop until they had marched halfway across the ceiling. A massive bed floated outward from the windows and the city's night lights beyond them and was covered with a black velvet quilted spread. Two slabs of cream-colored marble served as bedside tables and held crystal lamps that looked more like pieces of sculpture.

She tried to imagine what the bedroom would look like in the light of day and couldn't. It seemed meant to be viewed at midnight while rain fell on the ceiling and streamed down the wall of windows. "This is your bedroom, isn't it?"

"It's yours tonight."

"It's breathtaking."

"I get a great view of storms and full moons."

"Where are you going to sleep?"

"Don't worry about it. I have a very comfortable place to sleep."

Not worrying sounded like a good idea to her. She walked slowly to the end of the bed. He had placed the small overnight bag he had packed for her there. Looking for something familiar to dispel her feeling of unreality, she glanced inside and saw her long ivory silk gown. It was one she rarely wore. Joy and Grace had given it to her on her last birthday, saying it was for when she got lucky and met that special man. She wondered where Colby had found it, but then recalled him saying he'd found it by itself in a drawer, neatly folded. Thank goodness, she thought. She wouldn't have been able to wear it against her skin if she'd thought the person who'd broken into her house had touched it.

She looked so lost to him as he watched her. So fragile. And he had a big problem. He'd thought he would be satisfied merely with getting her here, but now that she was here, he didn't want to leave her alone, even if he would be in the next room.

He came up behind her and stroked his hands up her arms. "You'll feel much better tomorrow, Noelle. You'll see. After a good night's sleep, everything will look more manageable. And you don't have to do anything alone."

She turned. He was so close, she caught the tantalizing scent of spice and musk. "You've been very kind to me tonight. You didn't have to stay with me until the police came, and you didn't have to bring me here. My house isn't your responsibility. I really appreciate it."

Noelle, vulnerable and in an appreciative mood—he couldn't think of a more dangerous combination considering the fact that he had to fight against his desire for her every time he looked at her. "I didn't do anything because I felt duty-bound, Noelle. I did it because I wanted to."

"As I said, you've been very kind."

He smiled, and when he did he saw her gaze go to his lips. He almost reached for her then. "You can think so, if you like."

She looked away from him. "They took exactly what the officer said they would. My television, stereo, VCR. I don't have a home computer. As he said—one-stop shopping."

He curved a hand beneath her jaw and tilted her face up to him. "Try to put it all out of your mind for tonight and get some rest. I tried to pack everything you need, but—" He couldn't help himself. He lowered his head and brushed his mouth across the softness of hers. The indrawn breath she took sent fire straight to his loins, but he forced himself to straighten away from her. "If you need anything, give me a shout."

She couldn't sleep. She lay beneath the glass roof, watched the rain, and thought about how she had felt when Colby's lips had grazed across hers.

Alive best described it. For that all too brief moment she had come alive. Did that mean she had been emotionally dead until his brief kiss? Or could she simply chalk up her reaction to stress? Lord knew, she had been under enough today. Simply meeting Colby could account for a year's allotment. He was a man who could pull strong emotions out of her whether she wanted him to or not. Even now, when he wasn't in the same room, she couldn't stop thinking about him. It even seemed she could feel the imprint of his body on the black silk sheets, and she could definitely smell his scent.

She swung her legs over the side of the bed, stood, and walked to the window. The rain that had seemed to come from nowhere this afternoon was still going strong. But the lights of the city managed to penetrate the rain and the darkness to shine into the room and give a soft illumination.

She heard the door open behind her, and glanced over her shoulder. Colby was walking across the room, wearing only his jeans—a virile, sensual apparition moving through the shadows toward her. She quickly looked back out at the Dallas skyline, but she felt the skin on her back warm as he came up behind her.

"Can't sleep?" he asked quietly.

"Checking on me?"

"Yes."

Heat skimmed up her spine. He was as elemental as the night sky around them, and she couldn't seem to help but respond to him. The knowledge gave an edge to her voice. "No, I can't sleep, but it's all right. You can't die for lack of one good night's sleep, you know."

"Is that right?" He placed his hands on her bare shoulders and began to lightly massage the tense muscles he felt beneath his fingers. His touch was firm yet gentle, and very experienced, and it brought all her nerves to life. "Is this part of the treatment?" She hated herself for asking the question even as she asked it.

"What are you talking about?"

She slowly turned, forcing his hands to fall away. "I'm talking about those times when you bring a lady here to your loft to spend the night. Do you give out massages if she can't sleep?"

"When I bring a lady here to spend the night," he drawled, "there is no sleeping." Even in the dim light, he could see the color flare into her cheeks. She tried to wrench from his grasp, but his fingers tightened around her arms, holding her still. "Hey," he said on a soft breath. "I said that because I knew it was what you expected me to say. I shouldn't have. The truth is, I've never touched a woman like I touch you."

She briefly closed her eyes, embarrassed. He was right, she thought. She had deliberately baited him. "I'm sorry. I shouldn't have said that. You're right, of course. I'm not in the same classification as your girlfriends. I'm only a client who was temporarily without a home for the night." She couldn't bear to see his expression—he was probably laughing at her—so she stared at the strong lines of his throat, then allowed her gaze to drop to the muscles of his shoulders.

His fingers flexed on her arms. Beneath his palms, her skin felt like silk. Lord, he would love to strip the gown from her body and *really* touch her until she grew hot and fluid beneath his hands. His groin grew hard just thinking about it. Heaven help him, this wasn't the right time. She had received not one but *two* bad shocks today, and he wouldn't let himself take advantage of her. But he had to correct her. "Noelle, look at me. Please."

She swallowed hard. "If you leave, I believe I'll be able to sleep now." It wasn't the truth, but she would rather lie in the big bed alone than have him stay and start to want him. And she was very much afraid she would do exactly that.

"In a minute. Look at me."

Slowly she lifted her head until she was staring into his eyes. And in the shimmering reflection of the skyline lights, she could see a fire flickering amid the green depths. The sight started a burning in her lower extremities over which she had no power. "What is it?" she asked in a whisper.

"Your name on the contract you signed with my company made you my client, but the minute I met you, you became much more."

"More?"

He lowered his head, bringing his mouth tantalizingly close to hers, and when he spoke, his voice was rough. "It took about two blinks of those beautiful brown eyes of yours for me to begin to crave you in the worst possible way."

His breath fanned over her lips, heating her inside and out. Without thinking, she went up on her tiptoes and lightly touched her mouth to his.

He could barely call it a kiss, but it sent a bolt of electricity scoring through him. Then she did it again, a feathery, weightless, incredibly sweet kiss that made desire rush to his brain and his loins. He forgot why he hadn't been the one who had initiated the kiss, he forgot why leaving had been in his mind only minutes before. He pulled her into his arms and brought his mouth hard down on hers.

She immediately softened. Parting her lips beneath his, she was consumed with a hot hunger that burned reason right out of her. It didn't matter. This was what she wanted—his tongue deep in her mouth, his hand caressing her breast, her heart beating wild and heavy. Her arms slid around his neck, and her fingers threaded into his hair. He tasted like desire. He tasted like need. And all she could think of was that she wanted more.

She pulled away from him slightly but then went back into his arms, molding herself to him in a closer, more intimate way, and her mouth fastened in a passionate lock against his. The yearning inside her held her in a powerful grip.

She was making it easy for him, too easy, Colby thought, taking her mouth once again and thrusting his tongue deep into its honeyed depths. And, dammit, he couldn't get enough of her.

Her anger at him that morning had been only a slight indication of the passions that lay beneath. Her lips burned him, her breast tempted him. He delved beneath the low neckline of her gown and took her into his hand. Her hardened nipple scraped against his palm, and suddenly he couldn't restrain himself. He shifted his position and, with hands beneath her arms, lifted her so that he could fasten his mouth onto that tantalizing nub.

Ecstasy wound through her and pooled between her legs as he sucked. Her head dropped back, and she moaned. She both heard and felt him take a deep breath, then he slowly lowered her, letting her body slide down his hardened body until by the time her feet were on the floor, she was already reaching for him, her lips parted.

But he stepped away, and she was left quivering and needy.

Her expression was bewildered. "Colby?"

One slim silky strap of her gown had fallen from her shoulder, and the ivory silk gaped low in a curve that exposed the delectable sight of her nipple. He couldn't look at her without dragging her down to the floor and taking her right there. He whirled toward the door, talking as he went. "It's been a crazy day, Noelle. I think it would be better for everyone concerned if you went to bed. I'll see you in the morning."

For long minutes after, she stood where she was, staring in disbelief at the closed door, her body throbbing, her reason returning slowly and painfully. Finally she threw herself on the bed and buried her face in the pillow, her hands clenched into fists beneath it.

Lord but she couldn't wait to see the dawn of the new day. Only then would she know for certain that this miserable, completely bewildering day was definitely over.

Five

The faint smell of coffee nudged Noelle awake. She pushed her hair away from her eyes and looked up, straight through the glass roof. *Sunlight.* Yesterday was officially over. It was a new day, and thank goodness the weather report Mort Seager had heard was wrong.

She lay there, waiting for the relief to hit her, but the ease of mind she had expected didn't come, and it didn't take her long at all to figure out why.

She still had the aftermath of yesterday to deal with. To be more accurate, *last night.* And *Colby.* The burglaries seemed the least of her worries.

She had known from the first that he was the kind of man she could be attracted to, and she had tried to proceed with proper caution where he was concerned. Unfortunately she hadn't foreseen a temporary lapse of sanity on her part. But how could she? Her conduct had been so unlike her.

She had no excuse for what she had done; she could think of no reason. Last night she had gone into his arms and lost her mind. If he hadn't been the one to pull back, she would have willingly made love with him.

Remembering, she flushed hot with embarrassment.

She couldn't fault Colby. *She* had been the one who had raised up on her tiptoes and kissed *him*. He had simply followed her lead. She threw her arm over her eyes, trying to block out the memory. It didn't work. Into her mind came the picture of how they must have looked when he lifted her and took her nipple into his mouth. Heat flashed through her, leaving her shaking.

She threw herself out of bed and went into the bathroom.

Fifteen minutes later she had showered and dressed in the tailored pair of black slacks and classic white silk shirt Colby had selected for her to wear. She wasn't certain where he had found the outfit, and she didn't want to know. Lord, it wasn't any wonder he had decided she shouldn't be left alone. She had been too addled even to pack for herself.

She pulled out the few cosmetics she carried in her purse and applied them—pressed powder, a feathery caress of blush, a light touch of mascara, a few strokes of a brow pencil, and finally lipstick. Then she stepped back to survey the results in the mirror and found herself addressing her image. "He probably doesn't think you have a brain in your head, and I can't say I blame him."

She made a sound of exasperation at herself, then glanced around her. She supposed she had put off facing Colby as long as she could. Carrying her overnight bag and purse, she walked out of the bedroom.

"Good morning," Colby said, setting aside his

paper when he saw her. He was sitting at a long cream-and-gold marble table that was two steps above the floor on a raised platform in front of a wall of windows. "I was wondering when you were going to wake up."

She put down her bag and purse and glanced at her watch. "It's not so late. I've got about an hour before I need to be at the shop."

It wasn't so late, he mentally agreed. It was simply that he had been so eager to see her. "Come sit down, and I'll make you some breakfast."

She walked slowly toward him, surreptitiously studying him. This morning he was wearing light brown slacks, a green shirt, and a bold geometric-patterned tie that she didn't really care for. Not, she reminded herself, that it mattered. And not that he didn't look absolutely great. She remembered Maureen's description of him as "a hunk." To her mind the one word didn't begin to describe him. He was so much more—a forceful, powerful, sexual male who could make her heart stop with only a look.

"No, thank you. I can catch something later. I'm going to call a cab and go home. May I use your phone?"

Her wariness was back, he thought with a silent curse. Though he'd half expected it, he had held out a small hope that she wouldn't regret what had happened between them. *He* sure as hell didn't. He only wished he had been able to extend the kiss to its natural conclusion of lovemaking. It had been excruciatingly hard to walk away from her, and even though he knew he had done the right thing, his body had paid the price as he had lain awake in the night, every nerve pulsating with need of her, every muscle throbbing. "There's no need for a cab. I'll take you when you're ready, but don't go yet. Come sit down and at least have some toast and coffee."

She hesitated, but only briefly. She had some things to say to him, and it would be easier on her if she went ahead and got it over with.

A place was set for her. She settled into a chair in front of it, and he poured steaming coffee into her cup, then took his seat across from her.

He leaned back in his chair and eyed her thoughtfully. Then his mouth twisted into a wry grin. "There's something you'd like to say to me, isn't there?"

She took a sip of her coffee, then somberly regarded the dark liquid. "I suppose it wasn't too hard to figure that out. It's obvious that I owe you an apology."

He blew out a long breath. "Lord, it's worse than I thought. Noelle, if you try to apologize, I promise you I will do something drastic."

She lifted her gaze to him, curious, because it sounded very much as if he had just made a threat. "Like what?"

"Like come across this table and kiss you until you forget all about how embarrassed you are about last night. Hell, I may anyway. I want to bad enough."

She held up her hand. "Wait a minute."

"No, you wait." He sat forward, planted an elbow on the table, and pointed at her. "You're embarrassed because you think you started what happened, but you forget that I had kissed you earlier, and you forget that I was the one who put my hands on you first."

She shook her head, her mouth set in stubborn lines. "Still—"

"And anyway, what the hell difference does it make who kissed who first, or who started what? It was going to happen sooner or later anyway."

"I don't agree."

"You can disagree all you want, but if you'll give a second of objective thought to the matter, you'll know I'm right. I told you last night, I crave you in the worst possible way."

"But you—"

"Yeah, I know. I walked away, but only because you were in a very vulnerable condition, and I didn't want to take advantage of you. *Don't* count on my chivalry lasting. In case you don't know it, you're capable of turning me inside out, until the only thing I can think of is how much I want you. Now with me feeling that way, how long do you think I would have been able to keep my hands off you?"

She stared at him, stunned. No man had ever talked so plainly to her. In her experience men usually covered up what they were feeling and what they wanted with game playing. But Colby laid everything on the table. She would have felt safer if he had played games with her. Games she could handle. "Look, I'm trying to apologize for what I—"

He moved, coming around the table and jerking her into his arms. And before she had a chance to protest, his mouth was on hers in a full, deep, fiery kiss. Pleasure exploded in her, flooding her with heat, and she sank against him with a help-less moan. His response was to gather her tighter against him and plunge his tongue even deeper into her mouth, a shocking, shattering, intimate act.

The need was instant; the wanting flared to unbearable proportions. Her nails dug into the hard muscles of his shoulders through the fabric of his shirt. She was lost in a world of heat and velvet of Colby's making, and she had no idea how she was going to find her way out. His freshly shaved skin felt soft and smooth and smelled of soap and of him. Desire boiled inside her, and she wanted him as she had never wanted another man. But . . .

She was emotionally stronger than she had been last night, her mind a trifle clearer. And she remem-bered all the reasons why she couldn't allow this to go any further. With a desperation equal to what she might feel if she were trying to save herself from drowning, she reached deep inside herself. Drawing on every inner resource she possessed, she wedged her hands between them and pushed against his chest.

He released her, took a step back, and pulled several deep, ragged breaths into his lungs. "Yes, Noelle?"

She could almost feel an electrical charge ema-nating from him. "That can't happen again," she said, then almost winced when she heard how shaky her voice sounded.

"Why not?"

"It's simple really—and it's nothing personal. I'm just not interested in getting involved, with you or anyone else."

"Is that a fact?" His eyes glittered dangerously. "Well, I'm sorry to have to be the one to break it to you, but we're already involved. And if you doubt what I'm saying, I'll kiss you again. You melt in my arms, honey, and you make me go up in flames. That means we're involved up to the tops of our heads."

She touched her forehead, then rubbed the side of her neck. Her skin felt hot to her touch, almost as if she were running a fever. "What can I say? You're right. For whatever reason, I do seem to have this unfortunate tendency to—"

"Unfortunate tendency? Uh-uh. That's one you'll never get me to buy."

She balled her fists at her side, furious not only with him but with herself, with their reaction to each other, and with the situation that had thrown them together. "Whatever, it's not going to happen again. Do you understand? I don't want you to kiss me, touch me, or anything else. It's that simple."

"Sorry, sweetheart, but there hasn't been one single thing that has been simple since I met you, least of all the way we can make each other feel." He took one big step, closing the distance between them. Cupping her bottom with his two hands, he pulled her against the hardened mound of his pelvis. "Feel that?" he asked gruffly. "*That's* what you do to me. And it's only going to get worse until I can get inside you."

A firestorm raced through her bloodstream, eating up her resistance as it went and draining her strength. Realizing she wouldn't physically be able to free herself from his hold, she reached for her rapidly fragmenting mental resolve. "Let me go, Colby."

Before she could draw her next breath, she was free.

His gaze burned her with its heat, but his voice was calm and quiet. "Fight it, Noelle. Fight it and see how far you get."

She escaped to the table and reached for her coffee cup. Amazingly her hand barely trembled as she lifted the cup to her lips, but inside she felt as if she were coming apart. Feeling stronger after several sips, she replaced the cup in its saucer and turned back to him.

"Look, Colby, I know you have to do a certain amount of investigation on my store's break-in because of the possibility that your system was the real target, but I think you've asked the twins and me everything you need to. And as for my house, as I said last night, it's not your responsibility. The truth is, I'm going to be fine. The damage at the store isn't even enough to file an insurance claim on, and as for the house . . ." Her voice broke. After a moment she tried again. "It's true it'll take some work to put the house back together again, but I can take my time and give it a good spring cleaning while I'm at it. So . . ." At a loss to know what else to say, she trailed off and gazed at him from beneath her lashes. She couldn't tell how her words were affecting him. He had folded his arms across his chest, and his green eyes seemed to be even darker than usual. She cleared her throat. "So, I don't think there's any reason why we should see each other again."

He didn't say anything for a minute. Then, quietly,

he asked, "Are you through? Have you said everything you wanted to say?"

Eyeing him cautiously, she nodded.

"And are you through with your coffee?"

She glanced at the cup. She had had only a few sips. "Yes."

"Then let's go. I'll take you home."

She wasn't sure what she had expected, but certainly not this rather abrupt dismissal. "Wait a minute. That's it? You're not even going to argue with me?"

"Arguing with you really doesn't appeal to me, Noelle. Kissing you again is an entirely different matter though. I can hardly stand to be within twenty feet of you without kissing you. Unfortunately we don't have time for what another kiss would lead to. When I make love to you, I want to have all the time in the world, because, honey, we're both going to enjoy the hell out of it."

"Damn you, Colby," she said, infuriated, "*take me seriously.*"

"Oh, I do. I take you very seriously. That's the whole and complete problem in a nutshell." He brushed past her to jerk his sports coat off the back of a chair. "I'll get your bag."

The silence during the ride to her house seemed powerfully loud to Noelle. And she couldn't tell if the din was coming from Colby's brain waves or from the thoughts in her own head. But she didn't try to talk to him, because she knew she wouldn't be able to make him understand.

How could she explain the turmoil of a two-year marriage that had left her so drained, she hadn't been certain she would ever regain her energy? How could she explain that she was afraid of any sort of relationship that promised to be volatile, as theirs most certainly did? The answer to both questions was that she couldn't.

She knew without even trying that she wouldn't be able to convince him of the truth of what she had learned from hard experience. He'd try to change her mind, and heaven help her, he might just be able to do it. But at the end, when they were both so tired they couldn't fight any longer, she would be left once again to pick up the pieces of herself and try to go on. The problem was, after a relationship with Colby, she was afraid there might not be any pieces left. He was able to stir emotions in her that her ex-husband had never even come close to evoking.

Colby pulled into the driveway of her house, coming to a stop behind her car. She reached for the door handle, but he put a firm hand on her arm, stopping her. "Do you want me to come in the house with you?"

Beneath his hand her skin heated. Volatile, definitely volatile. With them, emotions were always a breath away from erupting. "No."

"Are you sure?"

"I told you—I'm going to be fine."

He scanned her face, an effort to convince himself of the truth of her statement. He couldn't. "I have some things to do, but I'll be by your store this afternoon. But between now and then, if anything happens, or if you need me for any reason at all, I want you to promise me that you'll call."

"Colby, I told you—"

"I know what you told me," he said, his impatient, curtly spoken words cutting off hers, "but you remember what I told you. And while you're at it, try to understand that there's just no way you can stop what's going to happen between us." As if to prove what he had said, he leaned toward her and pressed a gentle kiss to her lips.

Instant desire rose swiftly in her, congesting in her chest and throat and threatening to choke her. Feeling completely helpless against him, she bolted from the car. Safely inside the house, she leaned back against the door and pressed a hand to her burning lips. Dear Lord, she was her own worst enemy. It wasn't Colby she had to fight against. It was herself. What was she going to do? What *could* she do? She responded to his every look, touch, and kiss, and she didn't seem able to control it.

No answer came forth to solve her dilemma. Slowly her heartbeat returned to normal, and wearily she pushed away from the door.

She picked her way through the clutter to her bedroom.

She replaced all the drawers in the chest and dresser, then picked up a big, armful of clothes, carried them out to her car, and put them in the trunk so that she could take them to the cleaners'. She decided she wasn't really up to doing anything else. Besides, she wanted to get to work. Working was how she had put herself back together again after her divorce. Today she was hoping that work would divert her enough so that she would be able to put Colby into some sort of emotional perspective.

She went back to the porch to lock her front door after her but grimaced at the futility of it. From her experience in the last twenty-four hours, security was an illusion. If someone truly wanted in a place, illegal entry could be accomplished with a minimum of effort and a great deal of success.

In a black mood she pulled her car door open, threw her purse into the passenger seat, and slid in. She inserted her key into the ignition, but then paused. A stereo cassette tape was lying on the passenger side of the floor.

How strange, she thought. She couldn't remember playing a tape last night.

She picked up the tape and swiveled to reach behind her for the cassette carrier she kept on the floor behind her seat. Except it was sitting on the backseat, open. And her tapes were spread out over the seat.

She frowned. Had someone come along and decided to look through her tape collection? As far as she could see, none of them were missing. Maybe the intruder hadn't liked her taste in music. On impulse she opened the glove compartment where she kept the usual things—a flashlight, a map, a purse-size package of tissues, and a small first-aid kit. Nothing was missing—but everything had been rearranged.

Nausea rose to her throat. She slammed the glove compartment closed and dropped her head onto the steering wheel.

Someone had searched her car.

First her store, then her house, and now her car.

Dear Lord, what was going on?

"I need to see Colby Brennan immediately," Noelle told the receptionist who sat at the sleek half-circle desk in the lobby.

The receptionist looked up at her, startled by her abrupt appearance and demand. "Do you have an appointment?"

"No, but I need to see him. Call him or tell me where he is. But do it *now*."

The receptionist eyed her with a suspicion that Noelle might have found laughable at any other time. For the moment, though, her sense of humor had disappeared. "Look, I'm not dangerous, nor am I carrying explosives. I'm just very, very upset. Call him. My name's Noelle Durrell."

The girl punched a button and spoke quietly into the phone. Within moments Colby was striding into the lobby, his expression hard and grim. With one look he took in everything about her—the paler than usual color of her skin, the haunted expression in her eyes—but without a word he ushered her into his office. He seated her in a chair in front of his desk, then leaned back against its edge.

"What's happened, Noelle?"

"Someone has searched my car."

"Are you certain?"

"Positive."

"Was it broken into?"

"I'm not sure. The door wasn't locked when I opened it this morning. I usually lock it, but there are times I don't, and I can't remember if I did last night. Colby, I don't understand what's going on, and I'm beginning to get frightened."

He exhaled a long breath. "I don't understand what's going on, either, but I plan to find out. And as for you being frightened, maybe you should be."

She tensed. "What do you mean?"

He took his time answering her. "Noelle, your house was trashed last night, and all that was taken was a TV, a VCR, and a stereo."

"What do you mean *all?* That's a lot."

"But if those things were all he was after, he didn't have to trash your house. He didn't have to go through all your drawers and pull everything out of your closet. Those things were in plain sight."

"No, I guess not," she said slowly. "I didn't think about it in that way."

"Of course not. You were upset, and rightfully so, but it's something we need to think about now."

She wasn't ready to face up to the significance of what he was saying. "Have there been any problems with any of your other accounts? Last night you mentioned my store could have just been a test run."

"No problems yet."

"Yet? Then you still think it's a possibility?"

"I can't afford to overlook anything, and that's why I have people covering that possibility. But I'm concentrating my efforts where I think the problem really is—you and something you have."

She couldn't remember ever being as frightened as she was at this moment. Her tongue flicked out to moisten her dry lips. "Maybe my three break-ins were a coincidence after all. And maybe whoever trashed my house was simply checking to see if I had anything else of value they could use."

"Maybe," he agreed.

"And there were other houses in the neighborhood that were burglarized."

"Yes."

"So that means my house wasn't the target . . . doesn't it?" Her uncertainty showed in the tone of her last two words.

"It's possible you're right. I hope you're right. But my gut is telling me different. And because it is, we need to go back to square one and look at everything again."

She stared at him, wanting to argue but unable to do so because she knew he was right. "It's just so hard for me to accept that someone is after me."

It was not only hard for him to accept, it was impossible for him to allow. "So far, it hasn't been you, it's been your store, your house, and your car. We have no way of knowing if he found what he was looking for, but this is a very determined man. If he didn't, he'll be coming after you next."

She paled. "That's crazy, crazy. I own nothing of any great value."

"You don't think you do, but you obviously have something that is of value to someone. Figuring out what it is will be the trick."

She leaned her head to the side and rubbed her forehead. "You've been saying he. How do you know it's one person? It seems to me it would have taken a whole gang to trash my house, then break into three other houses."

"Or *one* someone who's very good. I have no proof, but more and more I'm leaning toward one man, one extremely *good* man, who knows exactly what he's doing." She started to speak, but he cut her off. "If my theory is correct, he took the earrings, the cash, and the couple of pieces of costume jewelry from your store to make us think it was a regular burglary. Then he went to your house and took the TV, VCR, and stereo for the very same reason. And he hit the other houses in your neighborhood to make us think it was just part of the rash of burglaries that's been going on in the area. As the officer said, it's not unusual for that to happen."

She felt chilled. His theory seemed so incredible. She was an ordinary person, and things like this didn't happen to ordinary people.

He leaned forward and took her hand. "I know this sounds beyond your comprehension and scary as hell, and to be frank, it scares me too. But I can promise you one thing. Nothing, and I repeat, *nothing*, is going to happen to you." He paused. "That is, it won't if you do exactly as I say."

"What do you mean?"

"From now until we find this guy, you can't be alone, not even for a minute. I know you have to be at the store during the day, and that's fine. You'll have one or more of the twins with you, plus assorted customers, right?" She nodded. "And I'm going to assign one of my men to you."

"You mean like a bodyguard?"

"He won't get in the way."

She sighed. "All right."

He released her hand and straightened. "Good. That takes care of the day, and at night you'll be with me at my place."

"Wait a minute. . . ."

He held up his hand. "Save your objections, Noelle. Your place is not fit for you to stay at, and a hotel wouldn't be secure enough. As for the twins' apartment—if this guy comes after you, you don't want them in his way, do you?"

"You mean—"

"I mean he could easily hurt one of them trying to get to you."

She groaned and dropped her head into her hands. "This is an absolute nightmare."

"Don't worry. It's not going to last."

She lifted her head and looked at him, her brown eyes large and liquid. "You can't know that."

"This guy hit your store, house, and car in quick succession, Noelle. Right about now, he's got to be pretty damned frustrated. He's also got to be worried as hell that you've figured out what it is you have. If I'm right about all this, he'll make his next move pretty quickly. Which is all the more reason for you to do as I say."

She shook her head. "I don't know about staying at your loft again."

"It's one of the most secure places in town, Noelle, and you'll be very comfortable there."

She wasn't sure it was possible to be comfortable with Colby. There were too many charged feelings between them. Even now, when he'd told her someone was after her, she was supremely conscious of him as a very sexy, compelling man, not as someone who was trying to protect her. Her brow pleated as a sudden thought occurred to her. "Where did you sleep last night?"

"On the couch. The loft has another bedroom, but I didn't want to be too far from you in case you needed something."

Heat rose beneath her skin. "If I agree to stay at the loft, *I'll* sleep on the couch, and you can sleep in your bedroom."

"Nope. Sorry. I need to be between you and the entrance. The loft is secure, but as I said, this guy is good."

He watched the color drain from her skin as his meaning sank in. He was used to violence, but she wasn't, and he could only guess how hard it was on her to consider that someone was after her. He'd said all he knew to reassure her about her safety, but he knew one sure way to distract her from her worries. "The only other arrangement I would consider is that we share the bed."

Her eyes widened. "Share the bed? No way!"

He shrugged. "Think about it. With me beside you, you'd be one hundred percent safe."

The twinkle she saw in his eyes stopped the harsh objection she was about to make. "You have a very high opinion of your abilities."

He smiled. "Give me a chance to show you just how good I am."

Her eyes narrowed. She wasn't certain if he was talking about his bedroom prowess or his ability to protect her, and she didn't feel like asking. She glanced at her watch. "Oh Lord, I'm late. I should have been at the store five minutes ago."

She rose, and at the same time he stood. "I'll follow you in my car."

"Good grief, Colby. I'll be driving in traffic in broad daylight, and my shop's not that far from here."

"I'll follow you in my car," he repeated, his expression implacable.

When Noelle pulled into the parking lot, she saw Grace leaning against the front door of the boutique, chatting with a customer who was a regular. Sottise's little white body was stretched out in a patch of sunshine. She rolled her eyes. He might be a pedigreed poodle, but he had a lot of hound-dog tendencies.

As she got out of the car, Colby pulled his green Jaguar up beside her and rolled down the window. "I'll wait here until you're inside. If you've got any errands to do today, either put them off or give them to one of the twins to do for you. I've contacted my man, and he'll be here within ten minutes."

She wasn't used to having her freedom restricted, and the concept that someone might be after her was still hard to accept.

Some of what she was thinking must have showed on her face, because Colby added, "And don't worry."

She chuckled. "Right." Her small smile held equal portions of both amusement and bemusement. "Good-bye, Colby."

"See you later," he said softly.

When Sottise saw her, he jumped up and gave a yelp of joy. She lifted him into her arms and pressed her face into his soft fur. "Did you miss me?"

In answer he licked every part of her he could reach. He was wonderful, she thought. She got the same reaction when she came back in the house after taking out the trash as she did when she'd been gone overnight.

Suddenly she laughed, because she realized Colby wasn't going to be pleased. She had no intention of staying at his loft without Sottise.

Grace nodded toward Colby. "What's that all about?"

"I'll tell you when we get inside," she said wryly, "but you'll never believe it."

Six

The front door of the boutique opened, and the UPS delivery man walked in, carrying several packages. Out of the corner of Noelle's eye, she saw Dan Kuhlman tense.

Dan was good, she conceded, as she signed the UPS receipt and directed the delivery man to put the packages in the back room. As much as a man could appear unobtrusive in a lady's clothing store, Dan was doing it as he sat in the corner. Clean-cut and good-looking, he had needed only minutes to develop the knack of appearing as if he were waiting for his wife or girlfriend to come out of the dressing room so that he could pass his opinion on the outfit she had tried on.

Joy saw him as a challenge and set out to make him fall under her spell. Watching Joy work her wiles, Noelle judged Dan had lasted mere moments before tumbling. But there was also no doubt in her mind that his attention never strayed from her, the front door, and the customers. She had to admit that she felt better knowing he was there.

During a break between waiting on customers,

Joy waltzed up to the desk, a meaningful light in her eyes. "So, Grace tells me you spent the night at Colby's."

Noelle grinned. "Of course she did."

"She also told me the reason why you had to go there, and I'm sorry about your house, but since Colby's involved, it might all be for the best."

"I can't begin to imagine what you're talking about, Joy."

"It may be worth having your shop and house broken into."

"Trust me. *Nothing's* worth what happened to my house, and I'm not too thrilled about my shop being burglarized either."

With a frown that indicated Noelle obviously wasn't getting the point, Joy flicked a strand of long blond hair behind her back. "What I meant was—"

"Never mind, Joy. I *know* what you meant. But there's nothing between Colby and me. Last night he was very kind, but trust me, any continued involvement in these two cases is not because of me, but because of his business."

Joy's lips pursed speculatively. "He was kind, huh?"

"Kind." Not only that, she thought, he had controlled their potentially volatile reaction to each other. If he hadn't, she would have surely woken this morning beside him in his bed, smelling of lovemaking and him.

Heat fluttered in her stomach, but she ignored it. She was grateful to Colby, she told herself. He might be able to bring her alive with his kisses and make

her want him until her body was practically scream-
ing for him to plunge inside her and take away the
pain. . . . He might be able to. . . .

A wave of desire swept through her, and her hands
gripped the edge of the desk until her knuckles
turned white.

"I'm disappointed. I was hoping something wonderful would develop between you two. He's so nice,
not to mention—"

"Oh, look, Joy, Mrs. Miller just came in. Why don't
you go see if you can help her? Grace," she called,
"could you come here a minute?"

Grace walked over, tranquil and lovely. "What do
you need?"

Noelle picked up a fashion magazine and began
fanning herself in an attempt to cool herself off.
What she really needed was a nice arctic cold
front, but June arctic cold fronts in Dallas were
scarce. "Would you mind running a few errands
for me? You can leave an hour earlier than usual
for your classes today and do them on the way
to school."

"Sure, no problem. What do you want me to do?"

Noelle stared at her "To Do" list in front of
her, mentally sorting things that needed to be
done today from those things that could wait
until next week. "Let's see, make a deposit for
me at the bank—that's important—stop by the
veterinarian's and pick up a new supply of heart-
worm pills for Sottise—that's important—drop the
clothes that are out in the trunk of my car off at
the cleaners—that's *really* important—tell them I
need them as soon as possible, and, oh, take
that quartz necklace to the jeweler for repair

of the clasp—that's not so important, but I'd like to have it done. It's in my purse. I'll get it and my car keys, so that you can get the clothes."

A minute later she was handing the necklace and the keys to Grace, when Colby walked in the door. His gaze went immediately to her, then to Dan. Dan gave him a reassuring nod, and Colby headed for her.

Sottise, who had been having a little afternoon doze on his pillow, woke up, took one look at Colby, and began to whine.

Colby surveyed Sottise with narrowed eyes. "What's wrong with him? Is he sick?"

"No," Noelle said dryly. "He doesn't like what you're wearing."

He glanced down at his impeccably tailored slacks and sports coat. "What's wrong with what I'm wearing?"

Sottise's whining grew louder, and he buried his face beneath his paws.

Joy walked by, her arms full of merchandise retrieved from the dressing rooms, but she stopped and gave Colby a comprehensive once-over. "In my considered opinion it's the tie. Right, Sottise? The tie?"

Sottise's whine turned into a wail filled with misery.

Noelle burst out laughing. "It's definitely the tie. The geometric print is too bold. You need something more subtle."

Colby muttered some annoyed words in which mutt and some mild swearing played prominent parts. Nevertheless, he quickly undid and stripped the tie from his neck. With a scowl he stuffed it into his jacket pocket.

"There, there, Sottise," Joy crooned soothingly, "the bad tie is all gone."

A delicate shudder of relief shook Sottise's body, then he lifted his head and looked around happily.

"My niece picked out the tie for me," Colby said, skewering Sottise with a sharp gaze and roughly unbuttoning the top two buttons of his shirt. "It's always been a favorite of mine."

Noelle waved good-bye to Grace, who was walking out the front door. "I don't know what to tell you. Sottise is very good with ties. He's seldom wrong."

Colby stared at her, incredulous. "You *can't* believe that."

Joy interceded. "How old was your niece when she picked it out for you?"

"Five years old, and brighter than any mutt by a long shot."

"Obviously not, at least when it comes to ties. My advice to you is to wear it when you see your niece, but keep it in your closet the rest of the time." With a sunny smile Joy moved away, heading toward the front of the store to replace the clothes on their proper racks.

Colby looked at Noelle, and any further protest he was about to make died away. Her eyes were twinkling with laughter, and the sight nearly stole his breath away. "You are so beautiful," he whispered.

The compliment caught her off guard. "Uh, an investigative officer from the police department came by this morning. Since my house and store are within the same precinct, he's going to be on both cases."

He took her lead. "Did he have any new information?"

She shook her head. "He didn't even have the results of the fingerprinting they did here. He said it only takes a few minutes to run the prints through the computer, but that each case has to wait its turn, and it usually takes two to three days."

"That's right, but I called in a favor. The prints lifted from the jewelry cases were Grace's, and there were no prints found on your bedroom window."

She felt the hairs at the base of her neck rise. "That means . . ."

"It means we're going to proceed just as we planned." He glanced around. "Could we go back to your office? There's a couple of things I'd like to ask you in private."

She nodded. "Go on in. I'll join you after I tell Joy where I'll be."

"Dan," Colby called. "You can take a break. If you like, you can leave for lunch now. I'll stay here until you get back."

The younger man nodded. "Thanks, I'll do that, but I think I'll buy some takeout and bring it back here." With a glance at Joy he left.

When Noelle walked into her office, she found Colby sitting on the edge of her desk. Her office was relatively small, and being in such proximity to him sent her nervous system into a riot. She searched for something to say that couldn't be construed as personal. "Thank you for sending Dan over. His presence has made me feel a little easier."

Colby smiled. "I'm glad, but after seeing the way he looked at Joy, I've been thinking that I should have assigned an older man to the job, someone she wouldn't be tempted to flirt with."

"I don't think there's a man alive who would fit that description," she said wryly.

He shrugged. "Oh, well. Dan's trained in self-defense. I guess he can handle himself with her."

"I don't know. I'm not sure there's a self-defense technique discovered that could protect a man from Joy, but we'll all help him."

He chuckled, then his dark green gaze sharpened on her. "So, you're really all right?"

"Fine. It's been a very nice, ordinary day. The sun's even shining. It's hard to believe anything awful happened yesterday."

"Just remember how fast that rain came up yesterday afternoon, and don't be tempted to slack off on any of the precautions I've laid out for you."

She couldn't help but smile at the somber note in his voice. "Yes, sir. But please tell me," she said lightly, "how much is all this extra security you're giving me going to cost?" To her surprise his expression darkened.

"Do you really think I'm going to charge you?"

"Of course. Why wouldn't you?"

"Because, dammit, I'm not doing this for any business reasons, and if you don't know that—" He broke off and bit back a retort. "I guess you need showing— or I need to kiss you."

Quickly, smoothly, he came to his feet, pulled her into his arms, and crushed his mouth down on hers in a long, hot, hard kiss. When he ended the kiss and stepped away from her, her senses were swimming so badly, she thought she was going to lose her balance.

"Colby, you've got to stop doing that," she said breathlessly. "I told you I'm not interested in having a relationship."

He moved around her desk, quite deliberately putting it between them to keep himself from doing what he so badly wanted to do.

"Noelle . . ."

His voice was low and calm, but his gaze was so fiery, she thought for a fleeting moment that it might be able to pierce her skin.

"I'm about an inch away from losing my control completely. Now unless you want to end up making love with me right here and now, I suggest we change the subject." He pointed a rigid finger at her calendar. "Tell me about these men. This Gary. Who is he? What does he do? What's your relationship with him? And what about this Bill? I want to know the same things about him, plus all the others."

Hot and cold by turns, needy and angry, she practically screamed at him, "They are none of your damned business!"

"That's where you're wrong. If I'm going to be able to protect you, everything about you is my business, at least until I figure out what this guy wants and I'm satisfied that he's not a threat to you."

"I'll hire someone else. You're fired!"

"Gee, Noelle, I'm crushed."

"It's within my rights to fire you."

"You can do whatever the hell you want, but I'm staying on the job. Now tell me about the men that you go out with." He picked up the calendar and leafed through it. "You must have"—he paused to count—"*ten* different men listed in here. That's very impressive, Noelle. You're obviously very popular. I guess I don't have to ask the secret of your success with men, since I've been privileged to have a couple of close-up and personal encounters with you myself." His voice was silky. "Let's see, what does that make me? Number Eleven?"

Struggling with her temper, she said, "Last time I heard, being popular wasn't against the law."

"It depends on how you go about it."

"I'm sure my social life is no more active than yours."

"But then we're not talking about my life, are we? I'm not the one in danger."

She exploded. "And we don't know for certain that I am! This is ridiculous, Colby." She swept a hand toward the calendar. "None of those men would harm a fly, but you're just going to have to take my word for it, because I'm not about to tell you any more than that about them. They deserve to have their privacy protected."

He wanted to shake her. Heaven help him, he wanted inside her. "Loyal and passionate too. They're very lucky, but are they all lucky in equal measure?"

"What in the hell is that supposed to mean?"

"Is there someone special in your life?"

"*No.*"

He eyed her consideringly. The air was charged with so much tension, a lighted match would make the office explode. And he'd explode with a lot less incentive than a lighted match. He willed himself to relax and settled back against her desk again. "Answer my question."

"First answer one of mine. Is there someone special in *your* life?"

Her question surprised him, and his answer was harsh. "Do you really think I could kiss you like I did if there was?"

"It's hard to tell with some people. I have a friend who was engaged to be married. She thought her fiancé was madly in love with her until she found him in bed with her cousin the night before their wedding."

"Who said anything about my being in love with you?"

"My mistake." The two words were spoken softly, their tone hollow.

He wished for his words back. Under the circumstances not only was it the wrong thing to say, he hadn't meant it, he realized, stunned. *He was in love with her.*

The knowledge hit him like a blow to his solar plexus. His brain reeled as he sought to grapple with this astounding new information. He had never been in love before, but looking back, he was surprised that he hadn't realized it immediately. Yesterday he had looked into her brown eyes, spitting fire and anger, and his life had been altered forever.

"Colby?"

"What?" He focused on her and saw that she was looking at him, puzzled.

"Is anything wrong?"

Yes and no. Yes, because she didn't love him, in fact was trying her best to get him out of her life. And no, because how could he regret being in love with her? But he couldn't explain any of this to her. Later . . . later he would think about it and decide the logical way to proceed. Oh, right. Fat chance he could be logical about her.

He tried to get his mind back to the subject at hand. "Okay, if you're convinced there's nothing in the present that might be precipitating the trouble, what about something in your past?"

Her guard slipped instantly into place. "There's nothing."

His gaze sharpened. "You said that awfully fast. Maybe you'd better give the matter more thought."

"There's no need." She combed her fingers through her hair. "Look, I've said it before, and I'll say it again. Despite the series of amazing coincidences, all the trouble that's been happening can't have been happening because of me personally."

His eyes narrowed thoughtfully. "What's in your past that you're shying away from?"

"Nothing. I've got to get back out on the floor. Joy's probably got her hands full."

"Wait a minute, Noelle—"

But she didn't. With a curse he went after her, intending to bring her back into the office, but when he walked out, he discovered the store was full of customers. He made his way to Dan's side. "No matter what she says to the contrary, stay on the job and on the alert. I'll be back at six this evening to relieve you."

Dan nodded. "I'll be here."

"Good man." His gaze sought out Noelle. She was moving through the shop, carrying on conversations with several women at once. She was perfectly at home amid the silks and satins, baubles and beads—mysterious and alluring female stuff, guaranteed to mess with a man's mind and make him pray for relief for his body. As he watched her, she tossed her head and smiled at someone, and his gut tightened. Oh, yes. He was in love with her, totally and completely.

Colby was on the sidewalk when he heard his name being called. He turned and saw Joy.

When she reached him, she threw a furtive glance through the window of the store. "Good, Noelle's still busy. Listen, I just wanted to tell you not to worry about all those men in Noelle's calendar."

"How do you know I'm worried?"

"I heard you." She shrugged. "Actually everybody heard you. It was hard not to, you were both talking so loud." Her expression turned pensive. "It was interesting. I've never heard Noelle raise her voice to anyone before."

"What about the men, Joy?"

"Oh, right. You don't have to worry about any of them."

"Why not?"

"Because she only goes out with men who are interested in women only as friends."

Her meaning sank in. "Oh."

"Either that or she goes out in groups. If you ask me, her ex-husband has a lot to answer for."

He felt as if all the air had been knocked from his body. "*What?*"

Joy eyed him curiously. "I said her ex-husband has—"

"I heard what you said."

"But I thought you asked—"

"She's been married?"

"Yes. I thought you said you heard me. Are you all right? You look sort of funny."

His jaw clenched. "I'm fine. Thank you, Joy, for telling me. It explains a lot."

"Sure. I'd better be getting back in. Will we see you again today?"

He smiled. "You can count on it."

Thirty minutes before closing, Noelle found herself without a customer for the first time in hours. It had been a busy day, exactly what she had needed. She hadn't had time to think about whether or not she might be in danger, or to wonder what she could possibly have that someone else might want. Strangely enough, though, she had had time to think about Colby. In truth, he had seldom been out of her mind.

She rolled her shoulders, once again trying to shake off the thought and its implications.

Joy glided up to her. "Guess what Dan told me about Colby."

She eyed the young girl indulgently, not at all surprised that Joy had gotten Dan to talk about Colby. One look at Joy's lovely, friendly face, and most men would spill their guts. "Guess, Joy?"

"Well, okay, you don't have to guess. I'll tell you."

"I'm not sure I want to know."

"You do. Trust me. This is *really* interesting."

Of course she wanted to know, she thought, disgruntled with herself. The truth was, she was wildly curious about Colby.

She sighed, trying to give the indication that she was only obliging Joy by listening. Somehow, though, she was sure her attitude wasn't fooling anyone, least of all Joy. "All right, what did he tell you?"

"He told me how Colby got hurt."

All pretense vanished. "How?"

Joy's eyes gleamed with satisfaction. "There was a guy who had already killed a man and had been about to kill a woman. Colby chased him into an alley, and the guy turned on him with a knife. They fought, and the guy managed to sink the knife into Colby's leg. Colby was seriously hurt and bleeding badly, but he still managed to hold the guy until help arrived. Dan says that everyone who knows him admires him a great deal."

It wasn't a big thing, he had said.

"Anyway," Joy went on, "the injury was so bad, the doctors initially thought he was going to lose the use of his leg, but he fought. He sweated through months of physical therapy until he won back ninety-five percent use of his leg. Dan says most men would be satisfied with that, but that Colby still works out every day, trying for the last five percent. He won't give up."

Of course he wouldn't, she thought. She had been witness to his tenacity from the first. He hadn't merely filed a report and then left the case up to the police, even though she had asked him to. And when she had tried to fire him, he had informed her he had no intention of giving up until he had figured out what was going on.

She understood him a little better now and wished she didn't. He said he wanted her. That meant he wouldn't stop trying until he got her. A shiver raced through her, and she was unsure if its cause was fear or anticipation.

She was still trying to figure it out when Colby walked in the front door right before closing time.

"Are you about ready to go?"

She started to protest but stopped herself. He had already given her his reasons why she should stay with him, instead of at her house or with the twins, and even if she wasn't entirely convinced that someone was after her, he did make sense. She would never put the twins in a position where there was even a possibility that they might be hurt.

"Just about. What are you going to do? Follow me like you did this morning?"

"I'll drive you. It will be simpler."

Again she started to protest. He was threatening her independence, something that was very important to her. But once again he made sense. "Okay, but we'll have to stop by my house so that I can pick up a few things."

"Fine."

"And we'll need to load Sottise's pillow and blanket into your car. He'll need it tonight."

Hearing his name, Sottise came trotting up, his red-bowed ears perked with interest, looking from one to the other. "You mean Joy's car, don't you?"

"No. I want Sottise with me."

"Noelle—"

"My dog comes with me," she said, her tone implacable. "We're a package." Her set expression invited him to argue with her.

He didn't. He wasn't about to lose her company because of a stupid dog. "Okay, the mutt comes."

Joy, who had been unashamedly eavesdropping, clapped her hands in delight. "Sottise, you're going to get to ride in a Jaguar."

Even though he obviously had no idea what a Jaguar was, he appeared to as he wagged his tail in delight.

Noelle picked up one of the framed pictures that had been resting on a glass side table and studied it. The picture held two people, a stunning blonde and a darling flaxen-haired little girl.

"That's my sister, Kristie, and my niece, Rebecca," Colby said from the kitchen where he was cooking dinner.

Noelle was taking the opportunity to explore the loft, something she had been too shell-shocked last night to do. She had already discovered an office area secreted away on a second level reached by a circular stairway. By his desk a photograph of a group of men hung. It hadn't taken any detective work on her part to realize they were the policemen he had worked with before his injury. She found it interesting that he kept pictures of the people for whom he cared most out in the open.

"They're both beautiful," she said, staring down at the photograph in her hands.

"Thank you. I think so."

She eyed his wheat-colored hair, then looked back at the pair in the picture. "Blonds seem to run in your family."

He grinned. "That they do."

The next picture she picked up was of an older couple. The man was distinguished, the woman warm and motherly-looking. She held up the picture for his viewing. "Your parents?"

He glanced at the picture, then went back to chopping vegetables. "That's right. They're retired and live up at Lake Texoma year round. What about your parents? Where do they live?"

She replaced the photograph on the table. "I'm sorry to say they don't. They died when I was young. My grandmother raised me."

He straightened. "I'm sorry."

"It's all right. My parents' deaths occurred a long time ago."

"And you already told me your grandmother died six years ago."

"I did?"

"Last night."

"Oh . . . I don't remember."

"Do you have any family?"

"Cousins. Lots of cousins." She wandered over to the bar that separated the kitchen from the living area and perched on one of the barstools.

"Are you close to your cousins?" he asked.

She shrugged. "One or two more than the others." Sottise, she noticed, was sitting at the edge of the kitchen area, watching every move Colby made with keen interest. "Your food and water are over here,

Sottise." She pointed to the floor beside the bar where she had placed his bowls. He spared her a glance, then went back to watching Colby. "Have you fed him anything?"

Colby's face expressed amazement that she would even ask. "I thought you put dog food out for him."

"I did, but he lives in hope."

"He's just going to have to go on hoping, then, because I'm not about to give him any of our dinner. We're having steak."

"That's his favorite. Don't worry, Sottise," she said in a stage whisper, "you can have some of mine." Sottise wagged his tail in gratitude. She rested her elbows on the bar's counter and gazed thoughtfully at Colby. "You should get a poodle. You can obviously tolerate one, because we've been here for quite a while and I haven't heard you sneeze once."

He threw a disparaging glance at Sottise. "Just because I'm not allergic to him doesn't mean I would want him or anything that looks like him living with me."

She laughed. "You're funny. You're the only person who's ever met Sottise and not liked him. He's the sweetest dog imaginable. He was the runt of the litter, but when he saw me he wagged his tail so hard, he fell over, and I knew he was the one I wanted."

Her laughter warmed him. "That's because you obviously have a soft heart."

"Oh, and you don't?"

"Not even close."

"Oh, yeah? Then why do you have those crayon pictures on your refrigerator?" She pointed to the drawings, affixed by magnets to his cream-colored Sub-Zero refrigerator.

He glanced in the direction she was pointing, and faint color crept up his neck. "Rebecca did those drawings for me."

"So naturally you had to display them."

He stared stonily at her. "Yes, as a matter of fact, I did."

"That little girl has you wrapped around her finger, doesn't she?"

He went back to preparing the salad. "I have no idea why you'd say a thing like that."

"I don't either, unless of course it's because her crayon drawings are the one incongruous detail in a loft that would otherwise be a candidate for *Architectural Digest.* Or the fact that the only wardrobe misstep I've seen you make was because your otherwise impeccable taste was sideswiped by a tie she gave you."

"I *like* that tie."

A peal of laughter rang out from her. "I know. That's what I just said."

Seven

She was in big trouble, Noelle thought, as she undressed for bed that night. *Big* trouble.

She actually *liked* Colby, more with every new thing she learned about him. She loved the fact that he kept his niece's drawings on his refrigerator. She admired his tenacity, past and present. And as much as the loss of her independence chafed, she even liked the idea that he wanted to protect her. There was something very reassuring and gratifying about knowing he was keeping her safe.

This evening after dinner, when she had reached for Sottise's leash, saying that she needed to take him for a walk, he had taken the leash from her hand and with a scowl said that he would do it. Somehow the sight of the one very big, very disgruntled man and the one very small, very happy dog going off together had sent her into another peal of laughter.

She was in big trouble.

In some mysterious, insidious way her liking of him increased her wanting of him. Heaven help her, somehow desire for him had sunk deep into her bones like some alien virus and was refusing to go away. And she didn't think there was any cure. Or was the cure written in the heated air around her and she was just refusing to see it?

During the years following her divorce she had shied away from getting involved with any man who might be looking for a relationship. But why was she worried now? She certainly wasn't in love with Colby, and he had made it clear today in her office that he wasn't in love with her. As angry as she had gotten with him at times, there was no way she could ever say that he had led her on. No, Colby didn't play games.

She turned out the lights and walked to the wall of windows. Tonight the sky was crystal-clear, and the lights of the city were dazzling, each one twinkling and bright, like an earthbound star. Their illumination bathed the bedroom, creating a pearlescent twilight glow.

It was a breathtaking room and light-years away from the cozy bedroom she had created in her home, with its secondhand furniture, eyelet ruffles, lace pillows, and antique quilts.

She had seen Colby's bedroom during a rainstorm, on a sunny morning, and now on a clear night, and the room looked different with each change of light and mood. She liked it, just as she liked the man who slept here.

Oh, yes, she was in trouble. But, she told herself firmly, she could be hurt only if she allowed her heart to become involved.

She heard the door open behind her and turned.

Sweet heaven, Colby thought. He was in trouble. She was already undressed and wearing the silk gown she'd worn last night. He still clearly remembered that it had taken every ounce of moral fiber he possessed to make himself leave her. What was he going to do? How was he going to manage to leave her again, now that his desire for her had increased to unbearable proportions?

"I'm sorry to bother you," he said, a telltale trace of huskiness in his voice. "I just wanted to let you know Sottise has had his walk and is curled up on his pillow under his blanket, asleep."

She clasped her hands in front of her. "Thank you for taking him out. I would have done it."

"I told you, I don't want you out alone." He hesitated. Knowing what he should do and doing it were two entirely different things, and he wasn't at all surprised to find himself delaying the moment when he would have to say good night.

An emotion larger and more powerful than his willpower slowly impelled him across the room to her. "I meant to tell you earlier, I had my men out talking to people today, both in your neighborhood and around the shopping center."

"Why didn't you?"

He shrugged and slipped his hands into his pockets. "I guess I was enjoying our dinner too much to bring it up."

She had also enjoyed the dinner. She couldn't recall a single important thing they had talked about, but she had found herself laughing a lot. "Were your men able to come up with anything?"

"They've found a couple of people who remember a car—a light blue late-model sedan, nothing distinguishing about it. Does it ring a bell?"

"No."

"Think about it for a minute. Think about what kinds of cars your friends drive."

She did, then shook her head. "No."

He grimaced. "It's not a good lead. Unfortunately no one thought it suspicious enough to write down the license number. It could even be a rental car, but don't worry about it. Something will turn up."

She wrapped her arms around her waist. "I hope so. I want this to be over."

A pain wrenched his insides, then he got angry at himself. Of course she wanted this to be over. What right-thinking person wouldn't? And when it was over, he'd see her again. Even if she wanted to end their relationship, he would find some way to change her mind. He would, because he had to.

Though he had known her only a short time, it seemed to him he had known her forever, and he refused to envision his life in the future without her in it—whether the future was next week, next month, or next year.

"Noelle, there's one more thing I need to ask you."

His careful tone alerted her. "You sound as if it's something that you're dreading asking."

His mouth twisted with a wry grin. "I am. Let's face it—you haven't exactly been thrilled with my questions up to now."

She moved, walking slowly down the bank of windows, her fingers trailing over the panes and the lights reflected in the glass. "I only object to those that deal with my personal life."

He followed her with his gaze, almost mesmerized by the way the silk of her gown cupped her breasts and moved against her legs. "Well, I'm afraid this question does just that. But, Noelle, it's necessary. We've covered your present; now I have to ask a couple of things about your past." He saw her stiffen. "I have to, Noelle. I wouldn't be doing my job unless I did. I might have been able to let it slide if it were only the store burglary we were dealing with, and your house hadn't been trashed. But it was. Badly. And there are only two reasons I can think of for someone to do that."

She stopped and placed her palms flat against the glass, seeking coolness. "What are they?"

"That someone was looking for something, and he wasn't certain where it would be. Now, you're not buying that theory because you can't think of anything you have that would be of value to anyone else. So that leaves one other reason we should explore."

"What?"

"That someone has a vendetta against you, and he's out to scare you or hurt you."

She shook her head, and her hair brushed over her bare shoulders. "Sorry, but I don't buy that reason either. There is no one in my life who would want to do either of those things, present or past."

"What about your ex-husband?"

Slowly she turned to face him. "Excuse me?"

"Joy told me."

"My, my. Joy was certainly a busy little bee today."

"Why do you say that?"

"Never mind." She frowned. "Look, I've told you before, there is no one in my past who would wish me harm, *especially* my ex-husband. He's been out of my life for five years now, or maybe it's six. I really can't remember. *That's* how far out of my life he is."

"Tell me about him. How long were you married?"

"You're not going to let this go, are you?"

"No."

She exhaled heavily, then turned and retraced her steps along the windows back to him. "We were married for two years. We married when I was a senior in college and he was in his last year of law school."

"What's his name?"

"Ed Temple. He's a lawyer, and he works in one of those buildings out there." She nodded toward the downtown skyline. "I haven't seen him since the divorce, and trust me, he wanted it every bit as much as I did. Durrell is my maiden name, and I took it back after the divorce. And that's *all* you need to know."

"No, there's more. You see, Joy said something that made a lot of sense."

"I can't begin to imagine what that might have been." She wasn't feeling especially charitable toward Joy at the moment.

"She said your ex-husband has a lot to answer for because you either go out in groups or with men who aren't interested in you as a woman."

"Last time I heard, Joy's major was business, not psychology."

"Like I said, it made sense. And I'll be honest with you, the reason I can't let it pass has nothing to do with the break-ins. It has to do with us personally."

She shivered, but when she touched her face her skin was hot. "Why do you always have to be so damned up-front and honest about everything?"

"Excuse me?"

"Nothing. Look, there is no *us*."

"I couldn't disagree with you more," he said quietly. "But at least what Joy said has made me understand a little better why you try so hard to keep me at arm's length. I think—maybe without you being aware of it—that you're burdening me with the psychological garbage of your marriage."

"I just love this," she said, her voice heavy with sarcasm. "I'm surrounded by pop psychologists. *Psychological garbage of my marriage?* Colby, that's the most ridiculous thing I've ever heard of."

"Then why are you fighting so hard against me?"

Her heart had begun to pound so loudly, she could barely hear herself think. "Pay attention to me! My former marriage has nothing whatsoever to do with us." She had said "us," she realized with something like despair. It was as good as an admission on her part that there was something between them.

Well, why not? she thought, suddenly weary. It was taking more energy than she could spare to continue denying it. She should just accept the fact and try to find a way to get herself out of this tangled web of a relationship that she was in with Colby.

He came up behind her and put his hands on her upper arms. Her skin was warm and silky beneath his hands. "Are you sure that what you went through with Ed has nothing to do with us?"

"Positive." The two relationships weren't even remotely similar. She'd been in *love* with Ed, and she most definitely wasn't in love with Colby.

He tugged her backward until she was leaning against him. "Good," he said huskily. "Good. That means there's nothing to stop me from doing this . . ." He bent his head and nuzzled his mouth against the curve of her neck. "Because you have no idea what you do to me. I couldn't stand it if you were hung up on another man."

A strange sort of physical weakness overtook her. She dropped her head back against his chest, exposing the smooth line of her throat to him. He lifted a hand to lightly caress her throat, while his tongue came out to do the same, trailing down the side until it reached the place at the base of her neck where her pulse was beating out of control.

Fire ignited in the pit of her stomach and flared between her legs. A thick sweetness crawled through her veins. Her heart beat even harder, faster. She had felt the same way last night when he had kissed her, she realized. He had made the decision to pull away then. That meant that tonight *she* had to be the one to make the decision.

And she was also aware that there was a time factor involved. Minutes from now she could be so lost in his embrace that she wouldn't be able to think. It was even possible that she had only seconds.

The tip of his tongue licked at the pulse point, and she felt her legs weaken.

"I want to do this to every square inch of your body."

His voice was little more than a growl, and it scraped along her nerves, bringing heat rushing to the surface. Need was coming alive inside her. Her growing passion was fed by the intensity she felt surrounding them, holding them in its ever-constricting grip. But then intensity had been with them from the beginning.

Gently he turned her around within the circle of his arms, then he claimed her mouth with hungry, demanding kisses, and she found it impossible not to respond. Winding her arms tightly around his neck, she sank against him.

His tongue tangled with hers, the contact raw and electric. Fires began to ignite throughout her body. She could feel pulsating need, knew that with every particle of her being she wanted him desperately. The pleasure his hands and mouth were giving her was incredible. Greedily she pressed against him, wanting even more.

Then his hand stroked down her spine to her bottom, rubbing and caressing. She heard herself moan, and at the same time she heard a faint, distant warning bell. Her control was slipping fast. Her time was quickly running out. She had to save herself.

"I want you, Noelle," he muttered hoarsely.

His words fanned the flames inside her. Soon, she feared, she would be completely consumed by them. But she couldn't stop, not yet. . . .

He shifted, spreading his legs and cupping the rounded curve of her buttocks. Applying pressure, he pulled her against him, fitting her to him so that his hardened arousal pressed blatantly against her pelvis.

In the heated corners of her mind her creative processes took flight. Unable to help herself, she imagined how it would feel to be filled by him, with him inside her, pushing hard up into her, and her body responded accordingly, crying out for the release only he could give her. *She had to make a decision.*

He rocked his pelvis against hers, simulating in a highly erotic, raw way exactly what he wanted to do with her. "Noelle, for Lord's sake, say something. *Talk* to me."

She could be hurt only if she allowed herself to fall in love with him, she reminded herself feverishly. She could go to bed with him, have sex, satisfy the desire that raged inside her, and still keep her heart intact. *She had to make a decision.*

She wedged her hands between them, palms flat against his chest, and, with arms that shook, pushed away from him.

"Noelle?"

His features were harsh with desire; his chest was heaving. Holding his gaze with hers, she took his hand in hers and drew him down to the bed so that they were sitting side by side. "Make love to me," she whispered.

With a broken groan he slipped off the bed to his knees in front of her and for a moment buried his head in her lap. The hot air of his harsh breath seeped through the silk of her gown to her skin. Giving a low whimper—a sound she had never before heard come from herself—she tangled her fingers in his hair.

Hearing the sound, he lifted his head and pushed the gown up until it was bunched as high as he could get it around her upper thighs. Then he gently spread her legs and bent his head to press his lips against the softness of her inner thigh.

A soft cry tore from her throat. "What are you doing?" Again she twined her fingers through his hair, holding on to him.

"I have to go slowly," he said, his voice muffled by the kisses. Her skin was heated silk, his insides were on fire. "Too much of you too soon / . . and I'll incinerate."

She could feel her breasts swell and harden, her nipples throb for his mouth. Could she survive something like this? she wondered helplessly. Could she survive this wanting, this incredible, monumental need that blocked everything out and left only the raw, pulsating feelings?

He switched his attention to her other leg, and this time his mouth went higher to the tight curls between her legs. The feelings were threatening to overwhelm her. She didn't know what to do to help herself. She ached all over, but especially under his kisses. All available heat had pooled there, growing hotter, increasing in pressure.

He slipped his fingers up into her, and strong waves of pleasure ripped through her. Shuddering, feeling herself falling, she thrust her hands behind her to brace herself on the bed.

Going slow was exacting a heavy price from him. There were so many things he wanted to discover about her, but if he didn't have her soon, he was going to explode. He pressed his thumb against the tiny inner kernel that was the center of her pleasure and heard her inhale sharply. "You're so sweet, so sweet. . . ."

Suddenly she arched her back and stiffened as convulsions of ecstasy tore through her body. Finally she went still in trembling wonder.

With a rough sound he surged to his feet. Hot, dark passion burned in his eyes as he gazed down at her. The straps had fallen from her shoulders, and the neckline had slipped down her breasts, exposing the tops of the full mounds to the tight buds of her nipples. Her eyes were closed, her head was back, and she looked lost in a world he had taken her to, a world he was anxious to share in a more intimate way, a world made up of passion and heat and the two of them.

With his knee on the bed and his hands at her waist, he lifted her, shifting her back onto the velvet cover so that the bed supported her full length. As she slid upward, the gown slid down over her breasts to her waist and then past her hips. He finished stripping the gown from her, and after hurriedly undressing himself, he joined her on the bed, lying beside her.

Her eyes were open, filled with fire and an aching longing as she watched him. "I'm tired of going slow," he muttered hoarsely. "I'm ready to go fast now."

"Thanks for the warning," she said, laughing on a soft breath.

Bathed in a twilight-colored light, her slim body looked almost incandescent, white satin against black velvet. Her hair was spread around her in silky curls. Her breasts were high and round and a perfect size for him to take into his hands. Her nipples were a soft rose and tightly beaded. He took one between his thumb and forefinger and tugged, then he did the same thing with the other.

"I want you in every way possible," he whispered hoarsely.

Her stomach contracted, and she moaned with pure pleasure.

Covering one breast with his hand, caressing it, he crushed his mouth to hers with a force more powerful than he had used ever before. He didn't want to hurt her, but at the same time he had an irrational need to consume her, absorb her, make her as much his as was possible.

And when he felt her hands behind his head, increasing the pressure of the kiss, he all but stopped thinking and let the demands of his body take over. He pulled away only long enough to put on protection, and then he was between her legs. He waited a heartbeat while her body adjusted to his weight, then he lifted his hips and plunged into her, burying himself entirely in the moist, welcoming velvet of her flesh. A deep, soul-satisfying sound of satisfaction escaped from him.

"Colby."

She spoke his name softly, her voice scratchy with need and desire. He began thrusting into her with deep, powerful strokes and going faster, ever faster.

Noelle had never known such pleasure, such intimate togetherness, and she was overwhelmed with the force of the passion. She moved with him, arching up to meet him, crying out. She gave in to his every wish, and at the same time he gave in to hers, seeming to know her wishes before she did, fulfilling them before they crystallized in her mind.

The pleasure built, intensified. She writhed beneath him, urging him to drive even deeper into her, to make his pace even faster. She felt as if she were hurtling along a dark tunnel of incomparable ecstasy, and Colby was her companion on the wild and joyous journey. A brilliant white light awaited them at the end of the darkness, and her need to get there was out of control.

She held tightly to him, somehow knowing that if she was to reach her destination, he was her only hope. And then she was there, being lifted into the white light as violent shudders of blissful, soul-satisfying release racked her body.

Moments passed. Then, with great reluctance, Colby rolled away from her, and she made a sound of protest. "I'm not going far," he murmured. "I couldn't."

She felt as lifeless as a doll as he maneuvered her body so that he could pull the covers down and then over the two of them. She stretched like a cat, then curled against his warm, damp body, reflecting in a dimly amazed way that she had just experienced more pleasure with Colby than she had in her entire marriage with Ed.

But the truth was, being in a combative marriage had left her too numbed for physical pleasure. Colby's first kiss had brought her alive, and now it was almost too late to remind herself of the need for caution. Almost . . .

"Colby?" His name came out on an exhausted breath.

"What?" He curved his arms around her possessively. He had never felt such a pure, powerful satisfaction.

"I . . . I just want you to know that I don't love you."

Colby stilled. It had sounded as if she were trying to reassure them both, but if that was what she was doing, it had the exact opposite effect on him.

Even after he heard the even breathing of her sleep, he lay awake. Those words had been her attempt at putting distance between them. He couldn't let it happen, yet he didn't know how to prevent it.

He was in the middle of a mystery constructed on two levels. The first level consisted of the break-ins of the two properties owned by Noelle—three if he counted her car. Other than the possible threat to Noelle's safety, he wasn't too worried about the burglaries. Sooner or later, he was confident he would figure out who had done it.

But it was the second level of the mystery that was the most important to him, the most compelling—the mystery of how to win, then keep, Noelle's heart.

One thing he knew for sure; he wouldn't stop trying until he had solved both mysteries.

Colby felt a soft, warm pressure on his bare chest. He attempted to ignore it, to sink back down into sleep, but something was willing him to wake. He did his best to fight against it, but too soon he found himself at the edge of wakefulness.

Slowly he opened his eyes and saw dark brown eyes staring back at him. Startled, he came completely awake. The room was bright with the dawn light, and Sottise was curled atop his chest, gazing down at him with a patient watchfulness.

He automatically reached for the silky arm beside him. "Noelle," he said gently prodding her, "your dog is sitting in the middle of my chest."

Sleepily she lifted her head, surveyed the scene, then dropped her head back to the pillow. "He wants out. I'll take him."

"He wants out? *That's* why he's sitting on me?"

"You're the one who took him out last night," she mumbled. "I guess he figured he'd try you again this morning. Besides, he likes you."

"Wonderful."

She rolled over and pushed her hair from her eyes. "Where did you put his leash?"

He sighed with resignation. "Never mind. Go back to sleep. I'll take him out."

"Are you sure? I'm used to getting up this early and taking him out."

"I'm positive. Dog, move."

Sottise seemed to know some resolution had been reached, because he leapt from Colby's chest. But when he reached the end of the bed, he stopped and looked back at Colby.

"I'm coming," he grumbled. "I'm coming."

Sottise set his tail to wagging so hard, the whole bed shook.

Colby dropped a kiss on Noelle's shoulder. "Go back to sleep."

With her body still exhausted from last night's lovemaking, she found it very easy to do as he said. When next she came awake, she was aware of a hand gently stroking her hair and the enticing smell of coffee. She stretched, opened her eyes, saw Colby bending over her, and felt a small shock of thrill. It was rather nice, waking up to see his dark green eyes looking at her, she thought lazily. "What time is it?"

"It's still early." He gestured behind him. "I brought you a cup of coffee. It's on the nightstand."

"Thanks." She started to push herself up, but then suddenly realized she was naked, and the events of the night before came back to her in a rush. Quickly she snatched the sheet to her breasts, but she found the cover wasn't nearly sufficient to make her feel shielded from him. And her physical nakedness was only a very, very small part of the problem.

During the night she had completely let her guard down with him, and it scared her to death. She had been a wild thing, twisting and writhing beneath him with total abandon, unable to get enough of him. Because of it, a panicky desperation had set in with the light of day, and she began to try to rebuild her defenses.

Holding the sheet to her, she sat up, stuffed pillows behind her back, then leaned against them. When she dared look at him again, she saw him watching her closely, *too* closely for her peace of mind. He was about to start in on her again with another line of questions, probing her life, trying to find openings, however small, that would allow him to slip beneath her skin and drive her out of her mind.

"So how was your walk with Sottise?" she asked, choosing a topic off the top of her head to buy herself some time. "Did you bring him back with you, or did you abandon him somewhere in the wilds of downtown Dallas?"

"He's safe and sound back on his pillow, asleep, no doubt dreaming of chasing rabbits or whatever it is that poodles dream of chasing," he said, a touch of disdain in his tone. "Probably teeny, tiny stuffed animals, because those he might at least have a fair chance of catching. They wouldn't run from him, unless of course they had batteries in them. *Then* he'd be in trouble. Honestly, he sleeps more than anybody or anything I've ever seen."

Good, she thought. She'd managed to divert him. Grateful for what she was sure would be only a respite, she reached for the coffee cup, brought it to her lips, and sipped. "He leads a very exciting life, and he has to keep up his energy. I mean, he lives in a land of giants, and we can do anything we want to with him."

"Are you kidding me? As far as I can see, he's got the giants in his life wrapped around his front paw. The worst thing I've seen you do to him is have those ridiculous bows put on his ears."

"He *loves* those bows."

"No truly macho dog could love bows."

She took another sip of her coffee. "Well, he's as macho as any dog, and he does. He's very selective about them too. He won't let the groomers put just *any* bows on him. Fortunately they always keep the very latest in colors and designs in ribbons in stock."

He stared at her with good-humored disbelief. "You know, it crossed my mind to find a trash can in some alley and stuff him in it, and I should have just gone ahead and done it. The city picks up the trash today, and even if they had skipped today, a good-sized rat would have carried him off before too long. I would have been home free. I want you to know I was definitely tempted."

With a grin she replaced the coffee cup on the bedside table. "You were not."

"How do you know?"

"Because it would go against your nature to desert anything, no matter what it was, as helpless and as sweet as Sottise."

He smiled slowly. "So you must think you know me pretty well."

"No, but I do know *that* about you. Come on, admit it. I'm right. You were not tempted, not even a little. And while you're at it, admit that Sottise is growing on you."

"Oh, no." He shook his head firmly. "Not on your longest day."

She reached for a pillow and swatted at him with it, managing to land a harmless blow on his broad shoulders. "Admit it."

Laughing, he ducked away. "*No.*"

She took another swipe at him. "Admit it!"

Hearing the commotion, Sottise came bounding in. He leapt up onto the bed and immediately began to jump against Colby, barking with all his might.

Noelle wiped tears of mirth from her eyes and aimed the pillow at Colby once again.

"*Hey*," he said, laughing even harder. "This is no fair! Two against one!"

"He thinks you're hurting me, and he's protecting me."

"Then you're in big trouble, because that thing couldn't protect you from a mosquito." The pillow came whizzing his way once again, and this time he ducked beneath it, grabbed her around the waist, and play-wrestled her away from the headboard until she was lying across the bed, and he was over her. Frantically barking, Sottise jumped on top of him.

"Call off your dog," he said, tickling her.

She was laughing so hard, she could barely talk. Sottise was like a whirling dervish, circling and leaping, each time his paws landing squarely on Colby's back, his bark high-pitched and angry. "Not until you say he's growing on you."

"Okay, he is . . . like fungus."

The laughter was beginning to make her sides hurt. She wiped a tear away and tried to get her mirth under control. "Sottise, *attack*."

Sottise pounced on Colby's head, which sent her off into another peal of laughter.

Colby simply picked the tiny dog off his head and reached his long arm over the side of the bed to set him on the floor. Sottise immediately leapt back on top of the bed and resumed his attack.

Noelle went still, suddenly realizing that the sheet no longer covered her. She was lying naked beneath Colby, and the weight of his hard body pressing hers into the bed was a potent reminder of the long hours of lovemaking they had shared during the night.

He looked down at her, hot, dark awareness burning in his eyes. "Are we through playing?"

"Sottise," she murmured, "that's enough." Sottise immediately quieted and sat down, glancing from one to the other of them, his little chest heaving from his exertion. She was still looking at Colby, caught by the fire in the depths of his eyes. "I guess I should get dressed . . . and go in to work."

He slowly shook his head. "I told you. It's early."

"But I—"

He captured her lips, drawing her down into the depths of a deep, hot kiss that sent her blood singing through her veins. She lifted her hips, arching against him, something that had become a habit in the night. She was soft, moist, ready for him, and he had done no more than kiss her. . . .

She felt a cold, wet nose against her cheek.

She broke off the kiss, turned her head, and looked into Sottise's big brown eyes.

"Tell your dog we'd like some privacy," Colby muttered, his mouth pressed against her neck.

"Sottise, get down. Go to your pillow."

Sweetly Sottise licked her cheek, then bounded off the bed. She heard his tiny claws clicking on the concrete as he trotted into the other room.

Then, without another word, without another thought, she wrapped her arms around Colby and drew his lips back to hers.

Eight

Jeans and a polo shirt? Slacks and a dress shirt? Colby stood in the center of his room-size closet that also served as his dressing room and stared blindly at the clothes hung along three long walls. Normally, he didn't give two seconds' thought to what he put on in the morning, but this morning was different.

He could hear the muted sound of Noelle's shower running in the other room; he could visualize the way her slim, silky body looked as the water sluiced over her; and he had to grit his teeth to help fight back the urge to join her.

Earlier, he hadn't been able to let her go. He'd prolonged their lovemaking, stretching out the pleasure and the tantalizing torment of anticipation until they both had been half-crazy. And then, after what had seemed like an endless span of time, the end had come suddenly in that hugely powerful, explosive way that happened every time with them. Standing there, thinking about it, made him tighten and heat all over again.

He wrenched a pair of jeans from a hanger and stepped into them, then tugged a blue-and-white-striped oxford-cloth shirt from its hanger. While he was buttoning it up, he caught a glimpse of something white out of the corner of his eyes.

Sottise. The dog was sitting in the doorway of the closet, intently watching him.

"I'm not taking you out again," Colby said firmly. "You're just going to have to wait until we leave to go to work."

Sottise's cotton ball tail wagged.

Dropping down onto a bench to pull on socks and boots, Colby muttered a mild oath. "You're pretty useless, you know that, mutt? Real dogs are hunters or watchdogs. Those kinds of dogs *deserve* the title of man's best friend. But you—I don't know. All you do all day is sit on a satin pillow and watch women parade around in different clothes." He looked at Sottise again. He hadn't moved, but his tail was wagging sixty miles an hour.

"Damn, I'm talking to something that's little more than a ball of fluff." Giving a disgusted snort, Colby surged to his feet and grabbed the first sports coat he saw. A brown tweed.

Sottise started to whine. Colby pointed a stern finger at the little dog. "Don't try to play those games with me, because I'm *not* playing."

The whine of abject sorrow grew to earsplitting proportions, and Sottise collapsed to the floor and shielded his eyes from the sight with his paws.

Uttering a colorful and completely original combination of obscenities, Colby set his jaw and resolutely ignored the racket. Putting on the sports coat, he walked to the mirror to check his appearance. Damn. The sports coat definitely was wrong.

He glanced at Sottise and saw that the dog had

rolled over on his back and had all four of his legs sticking straight up in the air as if he were dying.

For one insane moment Colby actually considered wearing the sports coat just to show the dog he couldn't be made to buckle under because of his stupid histrionics. Then he realized that *he* would be the one to suffer if he walked out of the loft wearing the jacket. Not only didn't the jacket look right, its winter weight was hot.

He stripped off the jacket, hurled it into a corner of the closet, and chose a double-breasted, lightweight navy sports jacket. Sottise viewed the new combination from an upside-down perspective since he was still on his back, but he quickly rolled over, sat up, and gave Colby a big, hearty three-bark approval.

Colby threw up his hands, refusing even to attempt the process of choosing a tie with Sottise present.

In Noelle's office Colby hung up the phone from checking in with a couple of his men and glanced at his watch. It was almost one o'clock, and he was still at Noelle's shop. But this morning, instead of simply dropping her off and leaving her in Dan's capable care, he had come in with her and sent Dan out on an assignment.

Sottise was curled up in the chair beside him, asleep once again. No matter where he had sat this morning, Sottise had decided he needed to be there too and had wiggled into the space beside him.

Tentatively, lightly, he ran his fingers across the little dog's back and was surprised at how soft his fur was. A burst of laughter out in the showroom caused him to jerk his hand away.

Noelle walked in, a smile on her face, and his whole mood lifted. When they had arrived at the store this morning, she had changed out of the slacks and silk blouse she had worn yesterday and into a narrow purple cotton-knit chemise, cinched at the waist with a wide belt. The short-skirted dress was part of the store's stock and outlined the curves of her body to perfection. Every time he thought of how he had explored those same curves with both his mouth and his hands last night, his blood grew hot.

"You look happy," he murmured. "Did you make a big sale?"

Her smile widened. "No, in fact I probably just lost money on a sale."

"How did you manage that? By the way, would you like to sit here?" He gestured to the chair behind the desk he was occupying.

Grinning, she shook her head. "Stay where you are. I wouldn't want to disturb you two."

He narrowed his eyes at her teasing, but he did it in jest. He loved her teasing, as he had loved it when she had hit him with the pillow this morning. Whether she knew it or not, it showed that she was becoming more and more comfortable with him. "From what I've seen, very little disturbs Sottise." As if to prove the statement, Sottise lifted his head, glanced from Colby to Noelle, then went back to sleep. "Anyway, tell me about the sale."

She perched on the front edge of her desk, angling her body sideways so that she could see him. "Do you remember Officer Hogan, the officer who was here the morning we met?" He nodded. "Well, he came in a little while ago, looking for something for his wife. It's her birthday next week, and he wanted an extra-special gift. But he was so funny about it." Her eyes sparkled. "The idea of sorting through all the dresses and lingerie made him incredibly nervous, and he didn't have a clue what size she wore. I had a customer, so I turned him over to Grace. Thank goodness she was able to put him at ease. Her parents were uncannily accurate when they named her. In fact, now that I think about it, they didn't misname Joy either."

"Then Hogan found something?"

"He found a terrific suit. His wife is going to be crazy about it, and I think it was sweet of him to put himself through the ordeal."

"So sweet, apparently, you gave him a good deal."

"I gave him a *tremendous* deal," she said dryly, "but he couldn't have afforded the suit otherwise." The phone rang. She decided to let one of the twins pick it up out on the floor.

"You may come to regret your good deed. Don't be surprised if half the police force shows up expecting similar deals."

She shrugged. "Well, why not? It's probably the least I can do. I've certainly given them enough work to do lately."

"Not *you*, Noelle. The person who did the break-ins."

"And speaking of that person, is there anything new? You've been back here on the phone for a while. I was hoping maybe something had shown up."

He pushed himself up from the desk, leaving Sottise the whole chair, and walked around it to her. "Nothing new. It's not like on TV. All crimes don't get solved in an hour, minus commercial time. But try not to get discouraged. Sooner or later, I'm going to figure this out."

She smiled. "I never doubted you would."

"Never?"

"Well, maybe at the beginning . . ."

"At the beginning you would have thrown me out on my ear if you could have managed it."

Her expression turned thoughtful. "Maybe I wouldn't have exactly *thrown* you out, but I did want you to leave."

"But I wouldn't go." He closed his hands around her upper arms and drew her to her feet. "And I still won't."

His mouth began to lower to hers. Automatically her lips parted. Then Joy practically stumbled into the room, her arms laden with plastic-covered clothes. "I picked up your cleaning—" Her eyes widened when she saw the two of them so close together. "Oh, sorry. I didn't know anything was going on." She smiled saucily. "If I had, I would have come sooner."

Noelle crossed to her and lightened Joy's load by taking part of the clothes from her. "Thanks for doing this. I rolled our extra rack in here for them."

As she was hanging up the garments, Joy threw a mischievous look over her shoulder at Colby. "Sorry."

He grinned. "Me too."

Finished, Joy looked at Noelle. "I've got some good news and I've got some bad news. Which do you want first?"

Noelle sighed. "I don't know. Lately the bad news has been pretty bad."

"It's not that bad. You need to come back out on the floor."

"And you think that's bad news?" Noelle asked, puzzled.

"Well, yeah. Because you'll have to leave Colby. But the good news is, a new group of customers has come in."

Noelle glanced at Colby and saw that he was smiling. "I think I'll be able to bear up." She put her hand on the younger girl's shoulder. "Come on, let's go sell some clothes."

Colby spoke up, stopping her. "Could you wait a minute, Noelle? Joy, she'll be right out."

"Right. Don't worry about a thing. Now that I think about it, I'm sure Grace and I can cope." She closed the door behind her, then almost immediately opened it again. "Sorry again, but I forgot to tell you something, Noelle. Grace took a call from the jeweler. He wants you to call him. And Mr. Seager, the foreman of the crew who's working at your house, called. He said to tell you they'll be able to finish by this evening."

"Joy, get out of here," Colby said, his tone mild.

"Thanks," Noelle said, but Joy had already shut the door again. She turned to Colby. "Okay, what is it?"

"Do you get to eat lunch?"

Her brow wrinkled. "You wanted me to stay behind

to ask me about lunch? I thought it was something important."

"First of all, I don't remember saying it was important. But second, lunch *is* important, and I happen to be hungry. I thought we could go someplace quiet—"

She shook her head. "You're going to have to go without me. I usually order from the deli down the street."

He would have loved to try to change her mind, but he didn't. As much as he wanted to have her all to himself, even if it was only for an hour, he sensed he had already pressed his luck in several other ways. And he was about to do it again. "There's one more thing." He pointed to the calendar on the corner of her desk. "If you haven't already, you should cancel this date with Bill for Saturday night." He leaned down to better see another date. "And here's David next week, and—"

"Why in the world should I cancel things that are happening next week?" she asked indignantly.

He straightened, and the expression in his eyes was dark and hard. "Because you're not going to be available."

"By next week? Of course I will."

"No."

"Be very careful, Colby. You're messing with my life, and you have absolutely no right."

She reached for the doorknob, but he caught her hand and swung her around. "What my rights may or may not be has nothing to do with what I want. And, Noelle, I want a great deal."

He pulled her against him for a long, searing kiss. He continued the kiss until she felt as if every hair on her head was singed and every bone in her body had melted. And when he finally finished, she could barely stand upright.

He stared down at her, his eyes glittering darkly. "I told you I was hungry." Then he opened the door and was gone, and she was left to pull herself together.

Sometime later that afternoon, Noelle paused for a moment to take a breath. It had been a busy, profitable afternoon.

Dan had come back from whatever assignment Colby had sent him on. With the other man back she had expected that Colby would leave. Instead, he stayed, sitting in the corner, talking with Dan, and every once in a while retreating to her office to make calls.

Not surprisingly, the ladies who came to shop preened and posed for the two attractive men, coquettishly soliciting their opinions, laughing like schoolgirls when the men paid them compliments. But no matter how involved in conversation with Dan Colby appeared to be, or how often he cracked jokes with the twins, or how outrageously he flirted with the customers, Noelle had no doubt as to where Colby's real attention lay. His gaze stayed on her, burning through her skin to her bones.

"I'm impressed," said Noelle, sitting at the cream-and-gold marble dining table with Colby later than evening. Dinner was over, but they had lingered, sipping at their wine and chatting in a casual, desultory sort of way. "You're a wonderful cook. Tonight's dinner was actually better than the one you fixed us last night, and that's saying a lot."

"Thanks," he said easily. "I picked up some things from my mother and sister. The rest I've learned on my own. I enjoy it."

"Funny, I would never have guessed that about you. I would have figured you were the kind of man to catch a burger at your local sports bar."

"I do that too, sometimes. Especially when there's a good game on."

"What kind of game?"

"Football and basketball mainly, but I like all sports."

That she would have guessed about him, she reflected. She hadn't needed to know him long to know that he was very competitive. She had an added, totally inconsequential thought: He was also maddeningly attractive.

She silently sighed. Light jazz played on his stereo system. The golden reflection of candle flames shimmered in the windows. The food, wine, and company were perfect. It had all the makings of a wonderful evening.

For anyone else.

Something was bothering her, nagging at her. It was as if her subconscious was trying to tell her something. The problem was, she had no idea what it could be.

"What's wrong, Noelle?"

His question startled her. Being the object of his intense scrutiny was more than unnerving, it was daunting. "I don't know. I'm not sure."

He sat forward, alert. "Have you remembered something, like seeing someone suspicious hanging around, or what you could have that someone else would want?"

She shook her head. "No. In fact, I'll probably go home tomorrow evening."

He was silent for a long moment. "I can't begin to tell you what a bad idea that is."

She fingered the stem of her wineglass. "I don't agree. Nothing out of the ordinary happened yesterday, at least it didn't after I discovered someone had been in my car, which most likely happened some time during the night. Nothing at all has happened today. I think it's all been a giant coincidence, that or the person's moved on to other prey."

"We can't be certain of that, Noelle."

She had no intention of giving in to him on this. Her reason for allowing him to bring her here to his loft had been valid at the time, but that time had passed, and she was feeling a real need to reassert her independence. "Maybe not absolutely certain, but reasonably sure. You said yesterday that you thought the guy would make his next move pretty quickly. Well, it's been over forty-eight hours, and he hasn't."

"Did you ever consider that maybe the reason he hasn't is because you've been well guarded every minute of that time?"

"Did you ever consider that I might be right?" she snapped.

"I considered it," he said, "but then I decided you weren't."

She took several sips of wine. As its warmth spread throughout her system, she tried to relax. Her nerves were strung painfully tight this evening. She felt restless, jittery, in fact almost panicky, and she didn't know why.

"Okay," he said quietly. "What about your house?"

"What about it?"

"Surely you don't want to go back there until we've had a chance to clean it up."

We. He'd said *we.* He was thinking like her protector, as if he had to be with her at all times. He made love to her at night and protected her during the day. He certainly gave his all for his job, and for some odd reason his dedication was beginning to chafe at her. "The twins have done a little work over there for me. The bed is remade with fresh sheets, and they've run several washer loads of clothes. They've also picked up a bit. It was their idea. They insisted."

"That was nice of them."

She nodded with a frown. "And the painters finished today." Seeking out a source of comfort, she looked for Sottise. He was asleep on his pillow. During dinner he had been sitting on the floor between their chairs, his whole attention on the food they were putting into their mouths. But now that Colby had cleared the plates, Sottise had lost interest in what they were doing.

"I ran a check on your ex-husband today," he said casually, almost too casually.

For a moment she thought she must have misunderstood him. "You what?"

"He's been remarried for two years now—did you

know that?" He paused, but try as he might, he could discern no emotion in her expression. "His wife is pregnant with their first child."

She pushed away from the table and stood so fast, her chair fell over backward. "What a despicable thing to do!"

She whirled away, but she had taken only a few steps before he caught up with her, closing his hand around her arm and stopping her in her tracks. "Maybe it is," he said, his face tight with controlled emotion, "but I do whatever it takes."

"Takes to *what*, Colby? Infiltrate and control my entire life?"

"I am not trying to control you."

"You could have fooled me!"

Alert to the distress in Noelle's voice, Sottise sat up, his little body coiled to spring into action.

Colby barely noticed. "I'm not going to apologize, Noelle. You told me he wasn't a threat to you, but dammit, someone out there is. And it's my job to investigate every possibility."

She shrugged away from his grasp, her nerves jangling out of control. "It's obvious we're not going to agree on this. I think it would be better if I went home tonight."

"*No.*" He caught her arm again and heard Sottise growl. He lowered his voice. "Come sit down. The coffee is made. I'll bring you a cup, and we'll talk."

"I'm tired of talking."

"Then *I'll* talk. Just come sit down on the couch with me. Please," he added, when she answered him with stone silence. Instead of waiting for her to say no again, he applied gentle pressure on her arm to guide her down the two steps of the platform and across the floor to the couch.

As much as she believed it best to leave, she found herself sinking down on the couch. He came down beside her, angling his body toward hers.

Sottise jumped up and settled himself between them.

"Get down, Sottise," she said softly. "Go back to your bed."

With a wag of his tail, he did.

Pressing fingers along her jawline, Colby turned her face so that she was looking at him. "Do you really think," he asked softly, "that given the danger I think you are in, I would leave any stone unturned? I had to check him out. But"—he paused—"I will admit that I had more than one reason. You once loved him, and I was curious." He grimaced. "Actually I was more than curious. I wanted to find out everything I could about him. You're a very guarded person, Noelle, but you chose this man to give your heart to."

"That was years ago, Colby," she said, puzzled and angry. "What possible difference could it make to you who I loved?"

"Because last night, right before you fell asleep, you thought it very important to tell me you didn't love me."

"I was trying to reassure you."

He nodded. "So I figured, but what I couldn't figure was why you were trying to reassure me, unless you were still hung up on your ex-husband."

"Colby, you're the one who told me you didn't love me, yesterday in my office."

"No," he corrected. "I asked you, 'Who said anything about love?'"

She waved an impatient hand. "It's the same thing."

"Not at all."

"Why not?"

"Because"—he exhaled a long breath—"you see, Noelle, I *do* love you."

She blinked, then very slowly, very quietly asked, "Why are you doing this?"

He had to smile. He'd never before told a woman he loved her. But in the past, if he'd thought about the possibility at all, and he wasn't sure he had, he supposed he would have imagined the woman he told would throw her arms around his neck and profess her love in return. Never would he have imagined Noelle's quiet horror. "I'm a simple man, Noelle. I have no hidden agenda."

She shook her head. "No way are you simple. I've never in my life known anyone harder to understand than you."

"Then let me repeat myself, and maybe this time you'll understand. I am totally and completely in love with you."

The full significance of what he was saying finally sank in, and she remembered what her first impression of him had been, that he was a man who wouldn't hesitate to take what he wanted whether it belonged to him or not. The panic rose in her so fast, it almost strangled her. She couldn't even speak. Once again she shook her head.

"Yes," he said softly.

A funny thing happened then. Something skittered up her spine—something like fear, something like excitement. No, it couldn't be excitement. She refused to let it be. She was afraid that it was. The fear pushed her to find her voice. "Well, I'm not in love with you. I'm sorry."

He'd known she didn't love him, but hearing her say it again hurt more than anything he'd ever experienced. "Don't be sorry. Just tell me why you think you're not in love with me."

At her side her hand balled into a fist. "Not think, *know.*"

He smoothed his palm across her balled fist until her hand relaxed, and he could thread his fingers with hers. "Okay, then, tell me why you *know* that you're not in love with me."

"Do you have to have it dissected? Can't you accept that I'm not?"

"No."

He was too close, too magnetic. She stood, pulling her hand from his, and without thinking about what she was doing, she set out on a wandering path around the loft. She'd never come across anyone like Colby. When he set his mind on something, he couldn't be put off. And though he might think she was guarded, she was finding it harder and harder to conceal anything from him. He was almost scarily straightforward. And he said he was in love with her. . . .

Suddenly she focused on her surroundings and found herself standing directly in front of him. She sat down on the black granite cocktail table, facing him. She felt a little better. The exercise and distance, even though both were relatively minuscule, had made her feel a little better. She had been able to fight out of his gravitational pull, and she felt stronger for it, strong enough to tell him why loving him would be impossible for her. "Ed and I dated for a year and a half before we married, and during that time we fought constantly. But we loved each other, and I guess we thought marriage would provide a magical solution. Unfortunately for both of us, the fighting only got worse."

"What did you fight about?"

"You name it, we fought about it. My working was one thing. Once Ed graduated, he got a good job, and he wanted me to quit mine. But that was the last thing I wanted. I had worked my way up from a sales position to being a buyer in a department store, and I loved my work."

"Did you ever think that the problem was that you were just wrong for each other?"

"Well, no kidding. Wrong with a capital W. We fought right up to our court date, and afterward neither one of us felt anything but great relief. The marriage left me exhausted. I think I might even have been on the verge of a breakdown. The only thing that saved me was my store. I concentrated on it, instead of my failed dream. Getting it on its feet helped pull me out of myself. It took me a couple of years, but I recovered, and I never again have any intention of allowing myself to become involved in a serious relationship. It's simply too exhausting."

"Allow yourself?"

She nodded. "That's right. Allow myself."

"But what if you can't help it? What if you meet

someone—say, me—and you fall in love before you even realize it?"

"It's not going to happen."

"What if it's already happened? Noelle . . . what if you've already fallen in love with me?"

"I told you, Colby. I'm not in love with you. When are you going to believe me? Besides, I would never fall in love with you."

"Why not?"

"The minute I laid eyes on you, I knew you'd require a great deal of energy, maybe more than I have, and I've been proven right. You and I have fought on and off ever since we met."

"*What?*" Completely surprised, he jerked, moving himself forward on the couch until he was sitting on its edge. He took her hand in his. She tried to pull away, but he didn't let her. "We've had discussions, Noelle. We've exchanged opinions, but we haven't fought."

"We're fighting now." Desperation tinged her voice.

He shook his head impatiently. "We're discussing our situation, and the fact that you can't see it means that I was right."

She looked at him blankly. "Right about what?"

"Your divorce from Ed *was* important to me. You've let it color your whole life."

She stared at him. Oh Lord, he was right! He had been through the kind of physical pain that changes a person's life, but he hadn't given up. Law enforcement wasn't simply his career, it was his life, and when he felt he could no longer do it to the best of his ability, he simply shifted into a different gear and kept fighting. Her divorce had put her through an emotional pain that had changed her life, but she had given up and turned herself in a totally different direction, away from relationships to her work.

She felt dizzy, confused. She wanted to lie down, close her eyes, and rest, and amazingly Colby seemed to read her mood.

He stood up and held his hand toward her. "Let's go to bed."

Automatically, as if she had been doing it every night for years instead of mere days, she took his hand. And though she wasn't entirely certain why, she went with him.

But the fact that she did bothered her, along with whatever it was that continued to roll around in her mind, creating a major disturbance.

Nine

Was it possible she was in love with Colby?

The question occurred to her some time in the night as she lay awake, staring up through the glass roof, and she had to wonder if she had finally stumbled upon what had been bothering her all evening. The subject was certainly enough to guarantee sleeplessness. But no . . .

It wasn't possible. It couldn't be. She refused to be in love with him.

They had made love several times during the night. His appetite for her had been strong, and hers had been a match for his. Each time, she had been swept away by the intensity of his lovemaking. Each time he had possessed her, turned her into liquid heat, taken her to undreamed-of heights, and in the end he had exhausted her. But still she hadn't been able to sleep. And so she continued to lie awake, watching the dawn gradually lighten the sky above her.

Time after time, she turned the disturbing question of love around in her mind in an effort to get a better perspective on it, but true perspective remained elusive. Over the years she had built a giant, impenetrable mental barrier against even the possibility of falling in love again. She couldn't understand why the question of loving Colby was troubling her. But it definitely was.

She turned her head along the pillow and looked at Colby, who slept beside her. His hair showed pale in the pearl-tinted dimness. His thick lashes showed as inky half-circles against his lighter-colored skin. A night's growth of beard shadowed his hard jaw. Those lips that had given her such pleasure were slightly parted. . . .

She returned her gaze to the glass roof above her, but even though he was no longer in her sight, he was still in her mind. His scent lingered on the sheets and on her body, and she knew without looking that there were places on her skin that still carried the marks of his desire. Even now, she knew that if he reached for her, she would go willingly and eagerly into his arms.

But there was more to him than his passion. She had seen his strength, his humor, and his gentleness. He was clearly a man to be reckoned with, someone she couldn't easily turn her back on. She could imagine eating pasta and watching *Casablanca* with him, but at the end of the evening it would be impossible to place a chaste kiss on his cheek, say good night, and then go to bed alone. No . . .

The muted clicking of Sottise's feet as he entered the bedroom interrupted her reverie, and she rolled over to the side of the bed. Seeing her awake, he reared up, put his front paws on the edge of the mattress, and looked at her expectantly.

"Do you want to go out?" she asked softly.

For an answer he wagged his tail with lightning speed.

She felt great relief. At last she had a valid reason to leave the bed with its scents and its temptation and to put some much needed distance between her and Colby. Hopefully the fresh air would clear her head. She slipped from the bed, quickly dressed, and, with Sottise on his leash, left the loft.

Colby came wide awake. For a few disoriented moments he couldn't decide what had woken him. Then an icy chill washed through him. Instinctively seeking Noelle, he flung his arm out toward her and, at the same time, rolled toward her side of the bed.

He was alone in the bed.

His feet hit the floor, and his hands reached for his clothes and his gun.

It was going to be a beautiful day, Noelle thought, following Sottise down the sidewalk. Already the horizon looked like a watercolor done in hues of pinks and oranges. With the light of day, she thought hopefully, surely her sanity would return. Maybe it had been the darkness of the night that had made her conjure up the distressing, untenable idea of love. With any luck the new day would banish the question from her mind completely. She just wished it would hurry and do so . . .

Sottise led her across an alley entrance and stopped at the corner of a building to investigate a particularly intriguing paper cup. Noelle stood patiently, gazing across the street toward the window of an art gallery.

Suddenly she was grabbed from behind, pulled deep into the alley, then pushed face-first against the rough brick of the building.

"Where is it?" a deep voice rumbled behind her.

Sottise immediately began to bark at the top of his lungs.

Surprised, afraid, Noelle tried to think. The coarse texture of the brick scraped the tender skin of her cheek. Her right hand was pinned against her back, but her left hand was free, and she tried to push against the building, but the man she couldn't see increased the pressure.

"Hold still," the man said coolly and calmly, "and tell me where you've got it. Is it up in your boyfriend's place? What the—"

She felt his body jerk, then heard Sottise give a yelp of pain. He had kicked Sottise, she realized with a wrench of her heart. She held her breath until she heard the barking resume. "Don't hurt my dog!"

"Tell me what I want to know, Noelle, or I'll do worse than kick the mongrel." His voice never once rose. It was as if he were asking her directions to the nearest library.

"What?" she asked frantically, struggling once more. "What is it you want?"

He jerked her pinned arm higher up her back. Pain stabbed through her, and she cried out. He threw the full weight of his body against her back, crushing her between him and the building. The air left her lungs, and for a few horrifying moments she didn't think she was going to be able to breathe again.

"Noelle," he whispered, his hot breath against her ear, "you've caused me a lot of trouble. Now you're going to hand it over to me, or I promise you I'm going to kill you *and* your dog."

Colby exited his building on a run, but once he reached the sidewalk, he realized he didn't know which way to go. *Oh, God, where was she?*

Then he heard it—the high-pitched, frantic, angry barking that he would recognize anywhere.

His heart hammering like a bass drum, he headed toward the sound, cursing the slight imperfection in his leg that made him a fraction of a second slower, but still moving faster than he had ever moved in his life.

When he rounded the corner, he took in the scene with one glimpse. A man had Noelle pinned against the building, and Sottise was a blur of white fur, barking and lunging at the man's ankle.

The instant Colby started for them, the man glanced around, saw him, and took off, running, down the alley. Colby took off after him, his gun drawn, but as he passed Noelle, he saw her turn and start to slide to the pavement. In Colby's mind it was no contest. He changed his course and headed straight to Noelle.

He reached her as her bottom hit the ground. Crazy with fear for her, he jammed the gun beneath his belt at his back and went down on his knees in front of her. "Sweet heaven, Noelle, are you all right?"

She gazed up at him, dazed and shaken, her cheek burning where the rough brick had abraded the skin.

He touched a finger to the spot and blotted up traces of blood with his fingertip. "Talk to me, honey. Are you okay? Did he hurt you?"

"I'm . . . okay. I think." She heard Sottise whimpering softly, felt him nuzzling her arm, and reached out to him. "He kicked Sottise."

Colby spared the dog a glance. "He looks fine, but don't worry. We'll have him checked out, right after a doctor tells me you're okay."

She pulled Sottise into her arms and held him gently against her. His whimpering stopped, but his tiny body was trembling, and his little red plaid bows were drooping. "I'm all right. Did you see the guy? Did you recognize him?"

"I caught only a brief look at him, and I didn't recognize him. Lord, if it hadn't been for Sottise, I wouldn't have gotten to you in time—" His throat closed, the thought so horrible he couldn't even finish it. "Did you see him?"

"No—" Her voice broke. "Colby, he was after *me*."

"What did he say?"

"He called me Noelle and kept asking me where something was, but he never told me what it was he wanted. He thought I knew what he was talking about."

Colby blew out a shaky breath. "He searched the three obvious places and couldn't find what he was looking for. I guess it was natural to come to the conclusion that you've hidden whatever it is."

"But I haven't hidden anything."

There was so much pain in her voice, he could hardly stand to listen. "I know." He stood and then bent to help her to her feet. "Can you walk?" She nodded, leaning against him and pushing her hair back behind her ears. "Are you sure?" he asked. "I can carry you." He might anyway, he thought grimly. He had the urge to pull her to him and never let her go.

"No, I'm okay. A little unsteady, that's all, but it will pass."

"Then come on. Let's see about getting you and Sottise looked at." Anger engulfed him. When he thought about what could have happened—that she could have been badly hurt or even killed— he wanted to tear Dallas apart until he found the man responsible. And if that was what it was going to take, then that was what he would do. But never again, he vowed silently, would he allow Noelle to be in danger, not even if he had to stay up all night and watch over her.

He lifted Sottise from her arms. "Let me carry him. He doesn't weigh much, but he weighs more than you should be carrying right now." The little dog gazed up at him with trusting eyes, then cuddled against him.

"Wait, Colby," she said, stopping after taking only a few steps. "I need to say I'm sorry."

His brows came together. "Sorry for what?"

"I'm sorry I left the loft without waking you up. My mind was on something else. I wasn't thinking. . . . You've said all along I could be in danger, but—"

"Don't," he said. "Don't put yourself through a wringer like that."

"But I should have listened to you."

He smiled, trying to lighten both their moods. "Remember that in the future, and think about this: We know one thing for certain that we didn't know before. You do have something someone else wants. Now all we have to do is figure out what it is."

She gave a small, hollow laugh. "Oh, is that all?"

"And you're really all right?" Joy asked Noelle anxiously.

Noelle smiled reassuringly. After making stops at an emergency clinic for her and at the vet for Sottise, she and Colby had just arrived at the store. Both girls had been waiting for them. Luckily no customers had come in yet, so they had the place to themselves, and she could talk freely. "Yes. The doctor was very thorough, but in the end, all he did was put an antibiotic ointment on my cheek."

"And what about Sottise?" asked Grace, casting a concerned gaze toward the dog. As soon as Colby had brought in his pillow from his car, Sottise had gone to it and curled up to rest.

"The vet said that he's fine too. He might have a little bruising, but it's nothing to worry about. If he seems sore, I can give him part of an aspirin. So far, though, he hasn't shown any symptoms. Colby's been holding him, and he hasn't cried once."

"Colby's been holding him?" Joy asked with interest.

"I didn't want Noelle holding him," Colby said, explaining. At the sound of the door opening, he tensed and swiveled, but he relaxed when he saw it was Dan. "I'm glad you're here. We have a lot of work to do today."

Colby filled Dan in on what had happened, then called the police. Officer Hogan arrived within ten minutes.

Noelle and the girls greeted him like an old friend. "How did your wife like her suit?" Noelle asked.

A faint blush crept up his neck. "She liked it a lot." He glanced at Grace. "And it fit great. Thanks for all your help." He turned to Colby and pulled out his notebook, all business now. "Even though the incident happened on another beat, I'm to take the report, since you're here in my area. You know, you really should have called it in at the time, and you should never have left the scene."

"I made the decision that it was more important to make sure Noelle was all right." His hard gaze defied Officer Hogan to tell him he was wrong. He didn't. "Anyway, I don't believe calling it in any sooner would get this guy caught. He's too damned smooth for that. I bet he's already gone to ground and is planning his next move."

"Did you get a look at him?"

"Only a glimpse, but I'll give you the best description of him I can. Later I'd like to come in and have a chat with a police artist. If we can come up with something, we can distribute the picture."

Officer Hogan nodded and began writing.

The day passed, much of it a blur for Noelle. Colby didn't leave. He turned the dress shop into a sort of command center, using the phone constantly and talking to an assortment of men who came and went. From her position in one of the store's most comfortable chairs, Noelle watched with bemusement as neither he nor the twins would let her so much as lift a finger.

Customer traffic was light, but she had no way of judging whether it was a slow day or potential shoppers were keeping away because of all the unusual activity in the place.

Joy and Grace fluttered around her like beautiful butterflies, fussing over her, bringing her tea and delicious treats from the neighborhood bakery.

After a morning nap Sottise perked up, and the twins fussed over him too. They cooed to him, telling him what a brave little dog he was, brushed his fur until it was as soft as down, and retied his bows. Once or twice Noelle could have sworn she even saw Colby slip him some food.

She had a lot of time to think, much more time than she really wanted.

Someone had threatened to kill her in an alley.

Someone was going to make another attempt.

Why?

She alternated between not believing it and being scared mindless.

And then there was Colby. He was totally focused on what he was doing, talking to his men, making phone calls, giving orders. But there wasn't a moment he wasn't aware of exactly what she was doing, and she knew it.

Last night he had told her he loved her. Later, she had wondered if she loved him. She still didn't know. Her life had been turned upside down in the last few days. Too much had happened. She didn't trust herself to know up from down anymore, much less whether she was in love.

By late afternoon she was tense and on edge, and her head was beginning to hurt.

"How are you doing?" Colby asked her, dropping down into a chair beside her. She'd been unnaturally quiet all day, and he was worried about her.

"Great," she said with false enthusiasm. "Just great."

"Okay. If you're up to it, I'd like to brainstorm with you for a few minutes."

"I said I was great." Her tone was strident.

"Right," he said. "Okay, well, I've been thinking about where this guy has searched."

"A better question would be what of mine hasn't he searched?" She picked up the telephone messages the twins had been collecting for her from a side table and thumbed through them. Mrs. Turner wanted to know if she could special-order a dress for her; the jeweler had called again, probably to tell her the necklace was ready; someone from Kenneth Kaye had called, probably trying to sell her their new line a representative for the Muriel Beachem sportswear line had also called, probably for the same reason.

He ignored her sarcastic tone. "The thing I keep thinking about is that he searched relatively *small* places, like your glove compartment, drawers, under your mattress. That could mean that whatever it is he's looking for isn't large."

She tossed the messages back to the table. "It could mean that, or it could mean that the man is simply psychotic and likes to tear things up."

"Try to think, Noelle. What do you have that is small that someone might want?"

"Sottise. Everyone who meets Sottise wants to take him home with them."

She sounded brittle enough to break. He leaned forward and gently touched her cheek. "Come on, honey. I know you've had a bad time, but I really need your help."

Tears sprang into her eyes. "I can't help you, Colby. I don't have *anything* . . ." She dropped her head into her hand. "I'm tired."

"Then I'll take you back to the loft." He stood. "Come on."

She lifted her head. "No. I want to go by my house this evening."

"Not alone," Colby said immediately.

She rolled her shoulders to relieve the tightness that had been forming in the muscles all day. "You can send a whole troop of Texas Rangers with me, I don't care. I just want to spend some time in my own house, surrounded by my own things."

Colby looked at her thoughtfully. "Fine. I've got to run downtown to the police station, but I'll drop you off. Do you have an extra key?"

"Yes," she said. "In my office."

"Good. Go get it and give it to Dan." He motioned Dan over. "Noelle's going to give you her house key. Drive over there, go through the place to make sure it's secure, then wait there. I'll give you about ten minutes, then bring her over. Stay with her until I get back. I won't be gone too long."

Dan nodded. "No problem."

• • •

Colby pulled to a stop in front of Noelle's house and noted with satisfaction that Dan's car was parked in her driveway.

Holding Sottise in her lap, Noelle turned to him. "I'm sorry, Colby. You're trying so hard, and I'm not being any help at all."

He lightly tangled his fingers in her silky hair. "It's all right. Sooner or later we're going to get this guy. You've just got to hang in there. I'm going to run down to the police station now and talk with their artist. We may be able to come up with a helpful sketch. It's only a matter of time." He reached over and rubbed Sottise's head. "I'll try to make it as quick as I can, but if you want to leave before I get back, Dan will drive you to the loft and stay with you until I come there. I also have a couple of other men watching the place."

"You think he'll break into your loft?"

"He'll try, but he won't make it. We're ready for him. And I promise you, no matter what, you'll be completely safe." He leaned over and placed a tender kiss on her lips. "See you soon." He slid out of the car and walked around to help her out.

She slipped out of the car, then put Sottise on the ground. Excited, he immediately headed for the house, but when he reached the end of his leash, he had to slow down and wait for her.

She had passed Sottise and was halfway to the house when she felt resistance against the leash. Surprised, she glanced back to see Sottise stopped in his tracks, gazing at Colby.

"Come on, Sottise," she said, gently tugging on the leash. But the dog wouldn't budge. What's more, he started to quietly whimper. She gave a laugh of amazement. "I don't think he wants to leave you."

Colby was standing by the driver's door, watching them over his car's roof. "I'm beginning to think he has good taste, after all."

"Sottise," she said firmly. "Let's go in the house."

But Sottise had stiffened his little legs into a locked position, and when she pulled on the leash, she ended up dragging him several inches.

She looked back at Colby, who was watching her with a smile. He was leaning against the top of his car, impossibly attractive with the afternoon breeze stirring the edges of his hair and a lazy smile gracing his lips. His white shirt was opened at the neck, and the shirtsleeves were rolled up several times, baring the muscled strength of his forearms.

It was only a moment freeze-framed in time, but it was all she needed, because suddenly everything became clear to her.

She loved him.

She felt a tug on the leash and glanced down to see Sottise straining against it to get to Colby, and she laughed out loud, happier than she could ever remember being. It seemed she and her dog were both in love with Colby.

She almost went back to him then, she almost told him, but he had someplace to go, and she wanted, needed, to keep the news to herself a little longer. Here she was, head over heels in love, and she needed time to adjust to the feeling, savor it. No, she would tell him tonight, when they had all the time in the world, and the sky around them was filled with lights and stars.

She scooped Sottise up in her arms, and with a wave to Colby turned and headed for the house.

She wouldn't stay long, she decided. She'd get Dan to take her to the loft so that she could have a long bath and maybe a short nap, and then when Colby came home, she'd tell him that she loved him. She could hardly wait.

Colby watched her walk in the door, then climbed into his car and drove away. He was deeply and totally in love with her, he thought. So much so, it had been hard to watch her move away from him. He'd wanted to run after her, stay with her.

With a soft chuckle he shook his head. "Hopeless, Brennan. You are hopeless."

And Sottise. He couldn't help but smile, remembering the little dog straining at the leash to get back to him, whimpering. He hadn't wanted to go with Noelle into the house. He had wanted to stay with him. . . .

His smile slowly faded. He couldn't remember Sottise ever disobeying Noelle. She had only to speak softly, and the little dog would immediately obey. But this time she had had to pick him up to get him into the house.

A chill went through him that left him shaking and sick at his stomach.

Something was wrong.

He sent the Jaguar into a skidding U-turn, narrowly missing an oncoming car.

Ten

Noelle shut the front door behind her, turned, and saw him. He had dark brown hair, cold, deadly eyes, and he was holding a gun inches from her head.

Sottise bared his teeth and began growling. She held him protectively against her.

With a quick wave of the gun he motioned for her to move. "Let's take a walk and put your dog in your bedroom. The man back there needs company, and I want the dog out of the way."

"*Dan*? You hurt Dan?"

He smiled coldly and pushed her forward. "Let's just say he's all tied up and taking a nap."

"What *is* it you want?" she asked desperately, walking in front of him. "Tell me, and I'll *give* it to you. Just tell me."

"I like your attitude, sweetheart. Continue co-operating, and this will go real smooth. Cross me, and I'll kill your friend, your dog, and then you."

He had said it as calmly as if he were reciting a grocery list, Noelle thought dazedly. Oranges, milk, and bread.

When they reached the bedroom door, the man said, "Open it real slow and put your dog inside, then close the door fast."

Her heart thudding, she opened the door and caught a glimpse of Dan, lying on the bed. She might have believed he was simply asleep if she hadn't seen the gag in his mouth, his feet taped together, and his hands taped behind his back.

She unhooked Sottise's leash to prevent him from getting tangled up with anything, leaned forward, and gently dropped him into the room. "Stay, Sottise," she said, then shut the door.

"That's a good girl," the man purred as he pointed the gun at her head. "Now let's go back into the living room and have a chat, and I'll give you a clue, it had better be a short chat."

Her legs were shaking. Hearing Sottise whining behind her didn't make her feel any better, but at least he was safe for now.

"Sit down," the man said, indicating a living-room chair, then perching on the arm of the sofa close by.

She sank into the chair. "Who are you?"

"It doesn't matter. Just give me the damned necklace, and I'll get out of here. It wasn't meant for you."

She looked at him blankly. "What necklace?"

The man was suddenly in front of her, shoving the gun under her chin. "Don't play games with me, Noelle. I don't have the time."

Fear had almost paralyzed her. "I-I'm not playing games."

"The *diamond* necklace. A mistake was made, and the necklace was put into the wrong shipment, your last shipment from Kenneth Kaye."

Her eyes widened. "I didn't get a diamond necklace, you've got to believe me."

His face split into a semblance of a smile. "Yes, you did. Uncut diamonds."

Gears in her head clicked into place. "You mean the *quartz* necklace?"

He nudged the barrel into the soft skin beneath her chin. "Whatever you want to call it. Where is it?"

"It's at the jeweler's. The clasp broke."

Seeing the man holding Noelle at gunpoint made Colby's blood run cold. He eased away from his position by the front window and made his way around the house, looking for a way to quietly enter.

At the back of the house he stopped and cocked his head at a sound. It was Sottise barking, he realized.

He crept along the house, following the sound, until he could peer into the bedroom window. Barking loudly, Sottise was alternately lunging at the door, trying to get out, and jumping on the bed to lick at Dan's face.

He saw Dan move; Sottise's methods were working.

Colby scanned the room, but he didn't see anyone else. Not knowing how much time he had, he set about getting into the house.

Thankfully Noelle hadn't thought about calling a repairman for either the lock or the window. The crescent-shaped cardboard he had put there following the burglary had been knocked out, indicating how the man had gotten into the house again.

Obviously he had waited inside and taken Dan by surprise.

Colby eased up the window. Then he was in. Immediately he went to Dan's side and stripped the gag from his mouth. Dan was awake.

"Can you stand?" Colby whispered, fishing his pocketknife from his jeans and cutting the tape binding Dan's hands and feet.

"One way or another," Dan said with a soft grunt, gingerly rubbing the back of his head. "I've got a knot on my head the size of a robin's egg."

Colby helped Dan to his feet and held him steady until he regained his balance. "How's your vision?"

Dan blinked. "It'll do," he said, in an equally quiet tone. "Damn, I'm sorry."

"Forget it. Where's your gun?"

Dan looked around him. "I don't know. He must have taken it. But, listen, I'm okay. I can help. Just tell me what you want me to do."

Colby glanced at Sottise, who had abandoned Dan to Colby's ministrations and was now devoting himself to hurling his body at the door, barking furiously. "Okay," Colby said. "This is the plan."

"You stupid bitch," the man said, his voice soft and devoid of emotion. "Now the jeweler knows too. I'll have to kill him."

"*No*," Noelle said, horrified. "He doesn't know. He couldn't." But he did, she thought. That was why he had been calling, wanting to talk to her. He wouldn't call her simply to tell her the necklace was ready. He'd given Grace a pick-up date when she'd taken it in. *Why* hadn't she thought of this before? she wondered with despair. "He was only supposed to work on the clasp, not do an appraisal."

"I hope for his sake you're right, but we'll find out when we go pick it up."

She swallowed and felt the barrel dig further into the delicate skin of her throat. "Pick it up? We can't. Not now."

His eyes narrowed. "Why?"

"Because he's closed. He closes his shop at the same time I do mine."

His lips curved upward, not pleasantly. "Don't worry. I can get in."

Suddenly Sottise came bounding down the hall, barking furiously, and when he burst into the living room, he headed straight for the man, his tiny teeth bared.

Noelle watched with horror as the man whirled, his gun aimed squarely at Sottise's small body. In the split second it took her to react, a desperate thought raced through her mind: Sottise would be little more than a munch of popcorn for a Doberman, and he was trying to save her from a man with a gun. She sprang up and forward and hit the man's arm. An explosion sounded in her ears as the gun went off, and then he hurled her to the floor. Frightened beyond belief, she searched for and found Sottise. He was alive and had his teeth sunk into the man's trousered leg.

She gathered her strength to lunge again when Dan charged into the room, drawing the man's attention to him and away from Sottise and her. "*Stay down, Noelle!*"

To her astonishment he threw himself to the floor and rolled forward toward the man's legs, and at the same time the front door exploded open, and Colby rushed in, gun drawn.

The man whirled toward him. Colby executed a hard, sharp karate chop to his arm. Just as the man yelled with pain and dropped his gun, Dan's body hit with a force that caused the man's legs to fold beneath him, and he crashed to the floor.

Colby dropped down beside the man and pushed the barrel of his gun beneath his chin, exactly as he had seen him do to Noelle.

"Give me a reason," he said, his voice as hard and deadly as the steel blade of a knife. "Give me a reason."

With one loud, angry bark Sottise jumped on top of the man, landing squarely on his chest with all four paws and the full force of his entire six pounds, corroborating in his own way what Colby had just said.

"So it seems your Kenneth Kaye was doing a booming illegal business on the side," Colby said to Noelle.

He had returned only moments before to the loft after several hours at the police station and had found Noelle in the bedroom awakening from a nap, with Sottise curled up on the black velvet quilted cover by her side. He had joined her, dragging pillows behind them until they were both propped against the headboard and Sottise was between them. Outside, the night sky had darkened, but the room glowed softly with the lights of the city and the stars above.

"Kenneth Kaye would set stolen gems in costume-jewelry settings to pass them off as fakes so that he could ship them out of the country without detection to dummy dress shops all over Europe. His contacts there would take the gems out of their costume-jewelry setting, cut them, and sell them as loose stones, or reset them and sell them as estate pieces."

She shook her head, still finding it all so hard to believe. "That's extraordinary. Kenneth Kaye is a well-known and respected person in the fashion world."

"He's still well known, but once the news gets out, he's not going to be respected."

"I don't understand. His line sold extremely well in my store. Why would he do such a thing?"

"The oldest reason in the world, honey. Greed."

"I suppose you're right, but what about this man you took in? How does he fit in? Who is he?"

"His name is Ralph Martino, not that it really matters. What is important is that he was Kenneth Kaye's partner in the illegal side of his business. I made a few calls while I was downtown, talked to him some more, and found out that he's responsible for several recent thefts of uncut diamonds that were being transported from South Africa to New York. He would steal the gems en route, and Kenneth Kaye would set them. I was right. The man's a real pro."

She sighed. "Thank goodness it's all over."

"I second that," he said with real feeling. He glanced down at Sottise. "Sottise, how would you like to have steak tonight?"

Sottise sat up and looked at him with interest.

"Trying to win my dog away from me?" she asked, teasing lights in her eyes.

He chuckled. "I seriously doubt that I could do that. No, as far as I'm concerned, Sottise is a genuine hero. He helped me save you twice, and I take back everything bad I ever said about him. He deserves a lifetime supply of steaks and bows, the bows subject to his approval, of course." He scratched Sottise's furry head, and Sottise licked his hand.

She gave a mock groan. "Sottise, don't be so easy. Make him work for your approval."

Sottise barked happily, somehow knowing there was something special going on and wanting to be in on it.

Colby laughed. "Being easy is a lesson I wish *you'd* learn from him."

"Oh, I think I've been plenty easy."

His brows raised. "Easy? You've got to be *kidding*. You've had me in agony since I first laid eyes on you." He leaned across Sottise and placed a tender kiss on her lips. Heat trickled into his bloodstream. He started to deepen the kiss, but then he remembered Sottise. The dog was still sitting between them, gazing from one to the other. "Do you think we could have a little privacy?" he asked the dog politely.

"Sottise," Noelle said, "go get on your pillow."

With obvious reluctance Sottise slowly walked down to the end of the bed, then stopped and glanced hopefully over his shoulder at them, apparently in case they had changed their minds.

"You can come back later," she said with a grin.

He wagged his tail, then jumped down and padded into the next room.

She looked back at Colby. "I don't know where to begin. You've been so good to me."

"Don't," he said warningly. "Don't even start."

"But there's something I need to say."

His expression was worried, but his tone was firm. "Before you say a word, you should know that I'm never going to stop trying to make you love me."

A smile hovered around her lips. "Tenacious."

"Damn right I am, and stubborn. Don't forget stubborn."

"How could I? Those are just two of the things I love about you."

He sucked in a breath. "You love—?"

"It's tempting to say I was slow to realize the truth, but in fact I really wasn't. A lot of things happened in a very short time, and it was taking all my resources just to cope. But there's no doubt about it. I love you."

"Thank God." He pulled her to him for a quick, fierce kiss, then gave a deep, booming laugh that made Sottise's ears perk up in the other room. "I can't promise our life will always go smoothly or that we're going to agree on everything. . . ."

"I never for a minute thought we would," she said with contentment.

"I'll live wherever you want," he said, thinking fast, trying to eliminate problems before they surfaced.

"My house would be too small for us." She glanced around her. "I think my things would look great in your loft. They would be an interesting contrast to what you already have here and would soften the place up."

"We can live here for a while," he agreed, "until we find a bigger place with a nice backyard for Sottise to play in, and then later on children. . . ."

She looked at him, her face aglow with love. "You're definitely going to take a lot of energy, Colby Brennan."

"Don't worry," he said with a growl, pulling her into his arms. "I'll make sure you eat well and take plenty of vitamins, plus spend a *lot* of time in bed."

She laughed happily, then fell quiet as his lips claimed hers.

And in the other room Sottise gave a blissful sigh, curled up on his pillow, and went to sleep.